Totally Bound Publishing books by Maggie Nash:

The Master's Prize
The Relic
The Dream Master
Kinky Bet
Crash and Burn
Summer Spectacles: Illuminations

I0571303

CRASH AND BURN

MAGGIE NASH

Crash and Burn
ISBN # 978-1-78430-815-5
©Copyright Maggie Nash 2015
Cover Art by Posh Gosh ©Copyright September 2015
Interior text design by Claire Siemaszkiewicz
Totally Bound Publishing

This is a work of fiction. All characters, places and events are from the author's imagination and should not be confused with fact. Any resemblance to persons, living or dead, events or places is purely coincidental.

All rights reserved. No part of this publication may be reproduced in any material form, whether by printing, photocopying, scanning or otherwise without the written permission of the publisher, Totally Bound Publishing.

Applications should be addressed in the first instance, in writing, to Totally Bound Publishing. Unauthorised or restricted acts in relation to this publication may result in civil proceedings and/or criminal prosecution.

The author and illustrator have asserted their respective rights under the Copyright Designs and Patents Acts 1988 (as amended) to be identified as the author of this book and illustrator of the artwork.

Published in 2015 by Totally Bound Publishing, Newland House, The Point, Weaver Road, Lincoln, LN6 3QN, United Kingdom.

No part of this book may be reproduced, scanned, or distributed in any printed or electronic form without permission. Please do not participate in or encourage piracy of copyrighted materials in violation of the authors' rights. Purchase only authorised copies.

Totally Bound Publishing is a subsidiary of Totally Entwined Group Limited.

If you purchased this book without a cover you should be aware that this book is stolen property. It was reported as "unsold and destroyed" to the publisher and neither the author nor the publisher has received any payment for this "stripped book".

CRASH AND BURN

Dedication

This book is lucky enough to be given a second life, and I want to thank all those who helped me achieve this. Firstly to Virginia and Venus for being awesome beta readers, and secondly to my amazing editor Sue Meadows for helping me make it a much better book than it was originally. I love you all!

Prologue

Sydney-Canberra Express
October 15th

In her hiding place in a dark alcove off the main walkway of the train, Beth Hamilton forgot how to breathe. The drama unfolding before her eyes starred a short, stocky man in a conservative suit, and from what she could see, he was in big trouble. Her suspicions were confirmed as another man pointed the barrel of a gun directly at his balding head.

Not your usual scenery for a train trip to Canberra.

Her throat closed up as she watched the gunman lift the mask he wore to reveal himself to his victim. Seeing his face, Beth closed her mouth, biting on her top lip to prevent any sound from escaping.

"You," said the bald man. "What do you want?"

The gunman smirked. "I want you to see the face of your executioner. You should have known we wouldn't let you get away with selling us out."

After bolting back to her own compartment at the scream that followed, she leaned against the door and willed her pounding heart rate to slow down. *Holy Cow.* All she'd wanted was to get a drink from the machine in the next carriage. Never in her wildest dreams had she expected to see a shoot-out.

Don't panic. They didn't see you.

Her gasps of air came in quick succession as she tried to think. She should act, but what could she do? The compartment was empty, except for some guy slumped in his seat, sleeping.

Should she wake him? She had no choice. There was no one else and no time. Either way, she couldn't just leave him there, not with a gunman so close by. She leaned forward and took hold of his shoulder.

He didn't react.

"Wake up," she pleaded as she reached for him again, this time more forcefully.

"What the—?" His eyelids fluttered as the no-longer-sleeping figure returned from the Land of Nod to the present. Beth watched as he woke slowly, blinking a few times.

She leaned closer to his face and shook him again. He smiled. A slow, sexy smile.

Holy cow. No man should be this good-looking. "You have to wake up *now.*"

As he caught her eye, he winked. "Well, you certainly know how to get a man's atten—"

"Just shut up and listen," she said, stopping him mid-word. *Why do men always wake up thinking of sex?* Although, with him, any other time… *Stop it, Beth!* She shook her head to clear her totally inappropriate thoughts and continued. "We don't have time. We're in danger."

He pulled himself up in the seat and bent his head from side to side, stretching the kinks out of his neck.

Who is this guy? Here we are in the middle of a crisis and he's doing his morning stretches? "There's a man out there—with a gun."

"And?" he asked, looking over her head to see what was happening behind her, as if he didn't quite believe her. Great, just her luck—a moron.

"And...he's going to shoot someone!"

He sat up even straighter, now wide-awake and finally, it appeared, all business. "Where?" he asked as he narrowed his eyes.

"Out there in the corridor," she pointed. At least he believed her.

The Hugh Jackman lookalike moved forward in his seat and whispered close to her ear. She noticed his spicy scent and tried not to think about how his warm breath sent tingles across her skin.

"Did they see you?"

"No, I don't think so," she whispered, as she shuffled backward, shrugging her shoulders in an attempt to throw off the tingling sensations coursing down her spine. "I hope not. I got out of there as fast as I could. Got any ideas as to what we should do?"

He nodded. "We need to contact the guard, but we definitely don't want to start a panic. You head the other way down the train, find the conductor and tell him to call the police, then move to a safer part of the train and stay out of sight."

Okay, not such a moron, but a macho chauvinist type. He strode in the direction of the gunman, but Beth stopped him by gripping his shoulder before she turned him around to face her. "And what will you be doing?" *Macho types aren't supposed to leave the damsels alone, are they?*

He pulled a face that told her she shouldn't 'worry her pretty little head'.

"I'm going to check out what's happening up ahead."

Not without me. "Neither of us should be going anywhere alone, not when there's an idiot with a gun loose on this train," said Beth, determined not to show how terrified she really was.

'Hugh' cocked his head to the side. "You said it yourself. We need to get help fast, so you go alert the conductor, and I'll go and see what's happening."

"What if there's another gunman back the other way? I've got a better idea," whispered Beth. "We both check out what's up ahead, then we both get the conductor." She lifted her chin and glared at the sexy stranger, daring him to disagree with her.

He narrowed those gorgeous brown eyes as he opened his mouth to say something, but then he paused. Shaking his head, he spoke, "I suppose that's a possibility. All right, we go together—but stay close and do what I say, okay?"

"Sure." *Anything not to be left alone here.* She nodded, and after a brief pause, he reluctantly moved toward the corridor, gesturing for her to follow him. As he edged forward, Beth walked closely behind him. The train swerved around a bend and she would have tripped if not for the hard male body in front of her, and the large hands belonging to said body that reached out to steady her. Her arms zinged from the contact and she instinctively moved backward, increasing the distance between them. *God almighty, this guy is a lightning rod!*

The rattle of the wheels bumping along the tracks competed with the pounding in her chest. When they reached the area where the two men were, he signaled for Beth to stop and crouch behind a seat. She slid into the space and cautiously peered out. Both men battled for control of the gun and from where Beth hid, it was definitely no contest. The gunman was taller, and from the size of the muscles in his arms, a lot stronger. It was only a matter of time before he overwhelmed the weaker man.

The gun went off. The shorter one grabbed his side where a dark red stain was rapidly spreading and, losing his balance, he fell through the open door to countryside below. The gunman straightened his clothes and adjusted his mask before casually walking over to the door, staring out while he replaced the clip in his gun.

Beth gasped.

The masked man turned back to the cabin and spied them both. He shifted quickly, striding toward them. 'Hugh' shoved Beth back toward the corridor, placing his body in front, shielding her.

"Get back!"

The gunman steadied himself, took aim and fired. Fortunately for 'Hugh', the jerking of the train around a bend caused him to lose his footing and the bullet missed its mark.

Beth bit down on her lip to prevent the scream that built up in her throat and slid back into the alcove of the seat, pressing hard against the wall, hugging her knees. A weapon... She needed a weapon. She scanned the limited space and spied a newspaper. She grabbed it then rolled it into a tight roll. It was better than nothing.

'Hugh' ducked and charged forward, diving at the gunman, grabbing for his feet. The gun went off again, but this time the bullet passed through the driver's cabin door, shattering the window in its path. The train lurched to the left as it rounded the next bend. The sudden movement had Beth hurtling out of her hiding place. She saw the two men struggling on the floor. The train jerked once more, forcing them closer to the door.

She jumped to her feet, her legs shaking as she inched closer to the fray. When the opportunity presented itself, she whacked the bad guy on the side of his head with the newspaper, but watched in horror as the movement of the train caused both the gunman and her cabin buddy to fall out of sight.

The train hurtled down the hill, increasing velocity until all movement stopped with a shuddering jolt. A deafening explosion sent Beth airborne before she landed hard on the floor. Shakily, she lifted her head and saw smoke coming from the gap under the door of the driver's cabin. She heard the tortured sound of a scream coming from a distance. It took her a few seconds to realize it was her own. Her head throbbed and her legs wouldn't cooperate when she tried unsuccessfully to lift herself up. Then it didn't matter anymore, as the world around her went black.

Chapter One

Beth jolted awake, the crumpled sheets damp and musty as she shivered in a pool of sweat. She attempted to shake off the haze of another nightmare, but the fear that had her stomach in knots was too much for her to go back to sleep. If only she could remember what the dream was about. She'd had the same one over and over since the train crash eight weeks ago. Now, home from the hospital, she'd hoped they would stop, but they hadn't—not yet anyway.

Her doctor had told her to give it time. *Easy for him to say*. It wasn't just the dreams. There was the concussion and the banged-up knee. Apparently bad dreams were common after any head injury, but after a severe trauma such as a train crash, they were almost a foregone conclusion. *Lucky me.*

Post-traumatic stress disorder, the psych team called it. *Yeah right*. Of course it was traumatic recovering from her injuries—and stressful? Definitely. Who wouldn't be stressed when they'd lived through an accident like that and had no memory of it? Not remembering wouldn't have been so bad, except for the fact that part of her subconscious must remember something and it was torturing her. Why else would she be having nightmares every night?

But time—and giving a name to her fear—hadn't stopped the feeling there was an important part of what happened that day that she needed to remember.

Something had definitely happened that day on the train, she was sure of it, and it had everything to do with how the train crashed. Why didn't anyone else seem to know? Certainly not the hospital staff, nor the police who'd been to interview her. Or were they hiding something?

The official report said the driver had suffered a heart attack and the dead-man's switch had malfunctioned. But if that was all there was to it, why were the detectives spending so many hours questioning her? *What aren't they telling me?*

She needed to know. If she could remember, the nightmares might stop and she could get on with her life. She threw back the covers then grabbed her stick before shuffling to the side of the bed to stand up. Her knee continued to be sore after the surgeon had repaired the damage, although the sharp pain had lessened after she stretched the stiff muscles. By the time she reached her bathroom, she'd forgotten the pain in her leg completely as her mind was elsewhere, thinking about the uncertainty of her situation.

She couldn't afford to wallow in self-pity, there were things to do, people and places to see, starting with an appointment with an old friend that she shouldn't miss.

* * * *

The silver-haired man sat and stared at his phone. He hesitated, taking extra time as he straightened himself in the chair. How was he going to fix the mess he'd gotten himself into?

He reached for the phone and his shaking hand punched in a long number from memory. A heavily accented voice answered on the first ring.

"Speak."

"She's left the hospital."

Silence stretched the moment, sweat tracing a path down his already damp neck as he waited for a reply.

"We expected this day would come. You'll have to watch her closely. Do you believe she knows anything?"

He dragged the crumpled handkerchief over his brow and blew out a breath before he answered. "I don't know for sure. According to my source inside the hospital, she has no memory of the train incident. We don't know if this is a cover or the truth. And if it is true, we have no guarantee that she won't get her memory back."

"Either way, we will need to watch her."

"Yes, of course. And if she does know something?"

"Eliminate her."

Eliminate her? Could he do it? He didn't know if he had the stomach for it anymore, but if it came to that, he knew someone who did — for a price.

* * * *

"Have you thought about what you're going to do next?" Dr. Bennett pushed his wireframe glasses back from the tip of his nose in a familiar gesture. "What about your studies?"

Beth smiled at the family doctor she'd known all her life. Normally she felt comfortable discussing her future with Dr. B. He was a trusted family friend, after all. But her University course could wait. It was an Internet-based course she could pick up whenever she wanted to, and she didn't feel quite ready for that right now. "I'm not sure what I want to do yet. I should probably think about going back to work first. The insurance payout won't be available for months yet and my bank balance is going to run low soon."

"Don't worry about that. You know I'll help you out with money anytime. You do need to get back to your usual routine as soon as possible, but you should wait for the leg to heal before you go back to work." Dr. Bennett's voice held genuine concern as he hauled his big frame across the floor to wrap his arms around Beth. She'd always felt safe in Dr. B's office. As a child she'd visited him often and had fond memories of him offering her jellybean bribes. The smell of the tan leather chesterfield brought it all back to her. But she wasn't a child with tonsillitis now. She was twenty-six years old and needed to stand on her own two feet.

"Yes, well, I don't have a choice at the moment. My boss has hired a temp for another month. I want to make sure that not only my leg heals, but I also get my head together in that time. I want to remember what happened. I'm sure I saw something important, and I can't move on until I find out what it is."

And there were those other dreams. The ones involving chocolate-brown eyes and a sexy smile that had her blood warming and her skin tingling. Of course she couldn't mention *those*, but it was a strange coincidence that they appeared the same time as the nightmares.

She moved out of the embrace and sat up straight, throwing her legs back over the side of the couch. "You know how it is when you can't remember an important detail. You can almost see it... It sticks up over the haze just a little, but not enough to recognize it completely. It stays on your mind and drives you crazy all day until it comes to you. That's how I feel all the time now."

"Beth," he said, leaning against the arm of the leather couch, "didn't your doctor tell you that you may never recover those memories? In cases of retrograde and anterograde amnesia, it's rare for the patient to get any of that memory back. It's the brain's way of coping with the pain. It doesn't want to remember, so try not to push it. It only makes it harder if you try to force the memories. Try to relax, and if they're going to come at all, they'll come on their own."

"I know, that's what my doctor said and my brain agrees with you, but I can't help wanting to know what happened. The dreams are awful. They scare me. I just want them to go away." Beth shuddered and pulled herself upright on the couch, folding her arms. "I've been thinking about going back to the scene of the crash to see if it triggers anything. What do you think?"

"You can't be serious?" He stepped back to the large chair behind his desk and sat down, his eyes wide with concern. "You're definitely not strong enough for that sort of ordeal, and it probably won't achieve anything anyway. Why don't you wait a while? When your knee's better, you might feel differently. I'll even come with you when the time comes, but I'm not convinced you're ready for that just yet."

"You think I should wait?"

"Of course I do. In my opinion, you're nowhere near ready. You'd be better off spending the time doing your therapy and catching up on your studies until then."

What a one-track mind he has, she thought, smiling. He'd been a wonderful support to her since her parents' death five years ago, but sometimes he acted as if it was his moral duty to keep her on the straight and narrow. Sometimes he forgot that she was a grown woman used to making her own decisions. Not that she'd ever been in trouble in the past, but she hated to disappoint him after all he'd done for her. "I suppose it makes sense to wait," she said tentatively, turning her head and biting down into her lip.

Maybe Doc was right. She would be better able to cope when her leg was stronger. She was getting more mobile every day, but she was still dependent on the stick. Although the pain wasn't as bad as it had been initially, the stiffness was still a handicap she didn't need. Maybe she *should* wait.

* * * *

By the time another week had gone by, waiting was the last thing Beth wanted or needed. Sleep only brought on the fearful dreams, so she'd started avoiding it altogether, finding numerous reasons to justify staying up later and later. The late night movies weren't doing it for her any more. She couldn't concentrate on reading and she sucked at knitting. And the worst of it all was that her health was beginning to suffer. She checked out her reflection in the bathroom mirror one morning after another sleepless night and she groaned. Her normally springy red curls were dank and limp, her skin was pale and pasty and the dark rings under her eyes made her look as if she'd gone two rounds in the boxing ring.

This could *not* go on. She needed control of her life. *Empowerment, that's what it's called.* Maybe retracing her steps would help bring back whatever pieces of her memory she'd lost and that would be the end of it. It'd only be an overnight stay. She could catch the nine o'clock train and be back by lunchtime the next day. She had no family to consider and Dr. B was the only person apart from her therapist who knew she was home. No one would even miss her. *Easy.*

* * * *

Easy? Standing on the cold platform at Central station the following day with her stomach in knots and her head pounding, Beth almost changed her mind.

Why is this a good idea?

Her breathing came in and out like an air pump, increasing in speed so that she was almost hyperventilating. What had she been thinking?

"Are you sick, miss?" asked the platform attendant. "You're not going to throw up, are you?"

Beth lifted her eyes from the ground she'd been staring at in an effort to staunch the growing dizziness her rapid breathing was causing. She would have fallen over if the attendant hadn't reached out and steadied her arm. "I'm fine really, thank you. I'll just sit down."

"Okay, if you're sure," he said as he guided her to a bench.

"I'm sure, thanks."

She sighed as he walked away. *This is ridiculous, I'm just catching a train. What's the worst that can happen?*

The worst had already happened, she told herself as she tried with every breath to convince herself not to

Maggie Nash

turn around and go home right now. Why was she putting herself through this again?

I might remember something. That could only be good, couldn't it? Beth continued the internal argument and at the same time fought a gnawing fear that was twisting, knot after knot, into her already fluttering stomach.

She jumped as the loudspeaker announced the train was about to leave. *It's now or never.* She dragged herself off the bench and hobbled into the closest carriage with her stick in hand and backpack slung over her shoulder.

* * * *

The lush green hills of the Southern Highlands should have been soothing. The quaint little townships they passed with their numerous antique shops should have stirred up at least some curiosity, but all Beth could see was a fuzzy blur as the train flashed quickly along the track. She sat with fists clenched so tightly that her knuckles were white and numbness was setting in. Despite the sun shining in through the window, she was shivering violently.

"Excuse me, but are you okay?" A rich, deep voice broke through her icy stupor and warmed her like smooth hot chocolate on a cold winter morning. She lifted her head to see who spoke and stared into the sexiest brown eyes she'd seen for a long time, maybe ever. *Holy crap.*

"I'm sorry. What did you say?"

"I asked if you're okay," the deep voice continued from the other side of the carriage.

Beth turned farther and inspected the face that came with the eyes and the voice. For a brief moment she thought she saw a flicker of recognition in his eyes.

20

Does he know me? Was he on the train that day?

No, that couldn't be true. What are the chances of meeting someone who had been on the train the day of the crash? *But he does seem familiar*, she thought as she shifted back in her seat and tried to place him.

"I'm fine, just a little travel sickness," she lied. "It happens sometimes. Maybe I should get a drink of water."

Beth fumbled with her stick as she tried to stand. The stranger also stood and put his hand out to stop her.

"No, don't get up. I'll get it for you."

Beth started to protest but it was too late. He'd already left the carriage. She sat again and tried to pull herself together. The train had traveled for over an hour now, which meant it wouldn't be long before they passed the crash site. Beth shivered at that thought. Except for her traveling companion, there hadn't been even one flash of a memory so far, and apart from this horrible feeling of fear and danger that she couldn't shake off, it could have been just any old train trip.

The stranger with the sexy voice returned with a cup of water and handed it to her. Their hands touched briefly, sending ripples of heat through Beth's fingers. She almost dropped her water but recovered quickly, hoping he didn't notice. He hesitated briefly before returning to his seat and resuming reading.

"Thank you."

"No problem," he replied, this time without even giving her a second glance as he shook the paper and turned another page.

Beth sipped slowly on the water, willing her nerves to calm down. What had just happened? It helped having this quiet companion to distract her from her fear, but when their hands had touched, it had been as if a fire had been ignited. She knew she should be concentrating on the journey, should be trying to discover anything that would help trigger her memory, but she couldn't help glancing again at this man. He was tall with wavy brown hair that was slightly long, falling over his ears. He was also gorgeous, she noted — no two ways about that. He smelled so good, all musky and virile male. She could still feel the heat rippling through her body from the brief touch of his fingers. She sighed as she tried to pull her thoughts back to her mission. He had an aura of calmness and strength that she found very reassuring, and for some reason, he made her feel safe. Safety in numbers, she thought. That must be it. It didn't hurt that he was a hunk, too. Nope, not a bit.

Daniel Wyatt stared blindly at the newspaper he pretended to read. The total lack of recognition in Beth's eyes left him positive now that the rumors of her memory loss must be true.

He dared not speak to her again. It was a risk and he may have already said too much. He couldn't risk her recognizing him.

Thinking back to when they'd first met, he smiled. He'd been sleeping—something he didn't usually do when traveling, but returning from a mission in London, he'd been exhausted. The train trip had been a way to get some rest before he handed in his report. He recalled seeing this gorgeous redhead with sexy green eyes leaning perilously close to his face and whispering in his ear. He'd thought he'd died and gone to heaven. Remembrance of the feel of her soft body colliding with his when they'd moved toward the gunman sent heat to his groin. He shifted in his seat to adjust his jeans. He could still smell her unique fragrance in his dreams. He couldn't allow himself that self-indulgence—not with what was at stake.

Shrugging, Daniel brought his thoughts back to the present. Yes, she'd certainly gotten his attention. She'd nearly gotten them both killed, too, but it hadn't been her fault. Just a quirk of fate, a matter of being in the wrong place at the wrong time. Like it or not, now it was his job to make sure she stayed safe.

He wondered why she was on the train. His department was keeping tabs on her, so he knew she'd only left the hospital a week ago. Hell, he'd only been back on assignment himself for the last two weeks. By the look of her tight expression and careful movements, she was still in a lot of pain.

Maybe she sought closure by returning to the scene of the accident. He hoped it was only that. For her sake, she would be better off never remembering. If only that gunman hadn't escaped, then she wouldn't be in the danger she was now.

He told himself that he shouldn't even be this close to her—should have been watching her from a distance. But when he'd seen how pale and scared she was on the platform, he knew there and then that he had no choice but to sit near her in the train. She was one gutsy lady. Not many would have done what she'd done to try and save someone's life, but she wasn't completely recovered and had no idea of the danger she was walking into. She needed someone to take care of her. From the little he knew about her, he feared she may take matters into her own hands again, and he couldn't allow it. Not this time.

Lifting his eyes from his newspaper, he surreptitiously took a peek at her long jean-covered legs and that gorgeous curly red hair. He sucked in a breath.

He couldn't let himself think about her in a personal way. She was a job, an assignment to complete. But reminding himself of that fact didn't help. He knew she'd already gotten under his skin. She haunted his dreams night after night—hot, erotic dreams that involved her and him, naked and sweating. She invaded his thoughts, and that was what worried him the most. He'd become too involved with a subject once before and had sworn he'd never go down that road again. It was too dangerous for both of them.

He would keep her safe, and the best way was to keep his distance. She was already in danger, even though she didn't remember anything. If she did recall what had happened, then the stakes would immediately get higher. Her life would be over unless the job got done with no emotional involvement. She'd better cooperate and stay out of trouble. It would be easier for both of them and much easier for him to stay detached. Just go in, do the job and get out with no complications.

Yeah, that'll work.

* * * *

It was time. Beth stood and braced herself for what she needed to do. The passage to the corridor was not easy. The space was small, making it difficult to maneuver her stick. The police report mentioned that the rescuers had found her close to the rear of the train, in the fourth carriage. She cursed herself for not boarding the train earlier so she could have seated herself in the same carriage where she'd been found. Making her way there while the train was moving was proving more difficult than she wanted. She needed to reach her target position before the crash site came into view, and her knee was already beginning to stiffen.

The journey was slow and awkward. The jerking of the train, especially around the many small bends, was not conducive to using a stick. She gripped the metal handles that rose above the backrests of the chairs, moving from one rung to the next to avoid falling on one of the few passengers who patronized this train.

Once she arrived at the fourth carriage, she leaned back against the wall and closed her eyes for a few seconds, letting her surroundings seep in.

As she opened her eyes and adjusted to the light in the carriage, she examined the dark blue seats. A few bags were scattered around, a couple of books and a folded magazine lay on the seat nearest the window. She guessed their owners would be in the lounge car having morning tea.

The sign for Mittagong station whizzed past. The train started to lurch roughly around a bend. Beth momentarily lost her balance and her stomach clenched as she struggled to steady herself.

Calm down. It was only a bend.

Only it could have been *the* bend.

She knew they were close now as she studied the map she'd taken out of her pocket. Taking a cleansing breath, she stared out of the window, conjuring images of what might've happened.

She spied another passenger coming into the carriage. He stared at her for a few seconds before walking straight past her and sitting down farther up the train. He probably thought she was mad, traveling around the train with her cane like that. She carefully scanned the carriage again to confirm she was on her own before she closed her eyes and concentrated once more. It didn't feel familiar at all. Something wasn't quite right here. Beth had a nagging feeling that this wasn't where it had happened. It just didn't *feel* right.

She made her way back down the train as quickly as her walking stick and injured leg would let her. She passed her own seat and noticed that her travel buddy was no longer in his place. She came to the first carriage and realized this was a more likely place. This was the carriage she would usually have chosen to sit. Funny really, she thought. She was always told that the rear of the train was the safest place to be in a train crash. But she liked the front. The ride was smoothest from there. It had come from years of travel sickness. It had used to drive her father crazy.

A quick movement behind her caused her to jump instinctively and turn around. Someone opened the door into the carriage behind her. A flash of memory hit her like a thunderbolt. Her head pounded and the breath *whooshed* out of her lungs. In her memory, a dark, shadowy figure was pointing a gun.

She could almost smell her fear as she froze in place. Her head started spinning and the taste of acid rose up in the back of her throat. Something whizzed past her head and her eyes were drawn to the hole it left in the wall beside her.

Bloody Hell! Someone's shooting at me!

Chapter Two

Beth started running as quickly as her stiff leg would allow. All thoughts of her injury were forgotten as she headed toward the driver's carriage. She'd almost made it when a pair of strong arms came out of nowhere and grabbed her, pulling her into a small cubicle and closing the door, locking them in.

A large hand covered her mouth as a voice whispered in her ear.

"Don't say a word, Miss Hamilton."

She struggled under the strong fingers that thankfully slackened their hold.

As the hand dropped, she turned her head around and was shocked to see that it was the man from her carriage.

"What the hell are you doing?"

"You were followed, and I had to get you out of there before they got you," he replied.

"Someone shot at me." Beth said. She swayed as a wave of dizziness hit, her heart pounding so hard her chest hurt.

He put his hands on her shoulders to steady her. "I know. There's no time to explain. We have to get off the train now."

"You know my name," she gasped as this fact finally registered. "And who are you to tell me what to do?"

"We don't have a lot of time. My name is Daniel Wyatt, and I'm with the National Crime Authority."

She glared at him, not really sure she'd heard him right. "Have you been following me?" Beth was angry, but she wasn't really sure why when it appeared this man was trying to help her. She really should've been scared shitless, but anger took her mind off the danger for the time being. "Is this about the train crash? Why don't you just ask me what I know? I can tell you right now. I don't remember anything!"

"Then why are you on this train, walking down memory lane and being shot at by dangerous men?"

Beth flushed. He had a point. "How do I know you're not one of them?" Beth narrowed her eyes at him, hating this feeling of being out of control. If she was honest with herself, she didn't believe for a minute that he meant her any harm. He was too cute. Cute guys weren't the bad guys, were they?

"Look. I can show you my identification if you like, but we don't have time. We've got to get off this train now, before they find us."

She didn't have much choice. Someone had tried to kill her and this man was offering her a way out. "Okay. You're absolutely right. I'm being a bitch and I'm sorry. What do you want me to do?"

Daniel visibly relaxed at her response. "Just sit tight for the next few minutes. I'll give you plenty of notice before we make our next move."

She attempted a smile in an effort to make up for her diatribe, although she wasn't sure if he could see her face anyway—which was probably a good thing given that she was scared to death and probably looked it, too. She peeked in his direction and saw that he was deep in thought. She took a breath and relaxed momentarily. There was nothing she could do right now, so she may as well conserve her energy.

Thinking about it, she realized that some good had come of this. Her dreams *did* mean something and she wasn't going mad after all. What Daniel had said to her just now proved that there *was* something behind her nightmares, and in a strange way she almost felt relieved. Maybe this guy could tell her more about what had happened on the train the day of the crash—help put it to rest once and for all so she could get past the nightmares.

"Farther up the track the train slows down round a sharp curve. We should be able to jump out safely there. Be ready."

"You know the track well."

Daniel lowered his voice. "I travel a lot. Now stop talking."

They both froze as the door handle turned. The cramped cubbyhole suddenly seemed even smaller. Beth held her breath. The seconds ticked away while she waited for the door to open. She couldn't see Daniel's face, but she felt his body tighten as he assumed the stance of a predator waiting to pounce. Thank God, he'd locked the door! He placed a finger over her lips, zapping them with sensation. The jiggling of the handle stopped and they both sighed in relief when the footsteps moved slowly down the corridor.

Daniel peered out through the door a few minutes later. "He's gone for now, but we'd better hurry." He led the way as they both scrambled through the connecting door leading to the outside of the train.

"On the count of three, we jump."

"I can't."

Daniel grabbed her hand and jumped, pulling her with him. "Yes you can," he shouted as together they became airborne.

Pain surged through Beth's injured leg as she landed. She rolled down an embankment, coming to a stop in front of the gnarled stump of a felled gum tree. Groaning, she dragged herself up into a sitting position, scanning her surroundings to search for Daniel.

The train was no longer in sight and the wide expanse of open land was bereft of vegetation. It struck her as sadly desolate. Appropriate really, since that was how she was feeling right at this minute. Where the hell was Daniel?

Her leg ached so badly that she bit her bottom lip to hold back the tears. *The damage better not be bad.* There was no way she going back to that torture chamber they call physical therapy.

She held her breath as she heard the scraping noise edge closer.

Daniel crawled over the rise and raised a hand in greeting.

"Oh my God, you scared me half to death! I thought I'd lost you."

"I was making sure no one followed us. I also picked up your walking stick."

"Okay. Thanks then."

Daniel shrugged and sat next to her, leaning on the tree stump. She could feel his body heat through her jeans and wriggled a few inches away from him, rubbing her knee to cover her action.

"Are you okay? How's your leg?"

Beth fell back against the tree trunk, lifting her hand to push her tangled hair out of her eyes. Her leg hurt like hell, but there wasn't much she could do about it right at this moment, so there wasn't much point in complaining. "Painful, but I can manage," she lied. "So what do we do now?"

"We get out of here as soon as we can."

"How do you propose to do that? You may not have noticed, but we're in the middle of nowhere."

Daniel pulled a mobile phone from his pocket and punched in a few numbers. "I'll get someone to pick us up. Then we need to disappear for a while."

What did he mean disappear? She couldn't just disappear.

Then again, as she'd realized before, there was no reason why she couldn't. She'd been alone when her parents had died and she'd gotten through that. She'd get through this. She made herself sit straighter and tried to maintain the distance from Daniel, ignoring the heat that was emanating from his direction. Not that it was working. She wasn't game to speak in case her voice betrayed the vulnerability that her proximity to him was causing.

Less than fifteen minutes later, the whirring of a helicopter broke the silence. Could it have really been only thirty minutes ago that she had been on the train staring out of the window, trying to conjure up images of the train crash? Everything was happening too fast.

The speed at which the helicopter arrived also both surprised and frightened Beth. How did Daniel have the resources to get a helicopter to them in this remote part of the country in such a short period of time? Whatever it was they *thought* she saw on that train, it must've been bloody important. Important enough to have people following and shooting at her.

If only she could remember. She had to think, but first she needed some answers. Daniel must've known something, but she sensed reluctance on his part to give her any information. She'd just have to make him. Ever since her parents' death, she'd taken charge of her own life. This dependence on someone else was an alien concept to her.

As the helicopter landed, Daniel helped Beth to her feet and collected her backpack.

"Keep your head down."

The touch of his strong hands around Beth's shoulders sent waves of heat across her skin. She barely had time to think before Daniel lifted her into the helicopter and buckled her in. By the time she remembered to breathe, he'd already moved into the seat next to the pilot, attached a headset and the copter had taken off.

The deafening noise of the rotors provided few opportunities for conversation, which suited Beth just fine. Her whole body continued to quake from the brief contact of being lifted into her seat. Talking was the last thing she felt like doing right now. Had he felt it, too? Did his body spark with energy? Were his senses on overload? Certainly Beth couldn't remember ever feeling so many sensations from so light a contact. Her skin tingled and the sensual heat continued to flow throughout her body.

What the hell is happening here?

She had been shot at, dragged off a train and whisked across the country in a helicopter with a man she'd just met. She needed all her wits about her. This wasn't the time to indulge in fantasies. He appeared to be on the up and up, but he still could be one of the bad guys. He hadn't been very forthcoming with information so far, and that was a worry.

She'd better ignore this attraction. Her life was in enough turmoil without sex clouding her judgment. It was probably the adrenaline rush anyway.

Who was she kidding? It was lust, pure and simple.

The five years since her parents' death had left her with little time for herself. Her parents hadn't been wealthy. The house and small insurance policy they'd left her weren't much, so it was still a struggle to make ends meet. Beth enjoyed her work at the art gallery, but it wasn't exactly a place to meet men. At least not straight men, she thought, smiling to herself as she visualized most of the management. Before the crash, her evenings had been taken up with study for her online computer science degree. In all of her twenty-six years, Beth had never had a serious relationship. She'd gone out with men, of course, but she'd never been able to let herself care too much for any of them. She had always held on to her independence. That way she could be the one to leave, not the other way around. But none of those men had ever made her sweat as much as Daniel did. God, just thinking about him made her heart race.

Although it made her feel incredibly alive, Beth instinctively knew she'd have to tread very carefully. She couldn't afford to let Daniel know what his presence did to her. Hell, he probably saved damsels every other week and walked away without a second glance. She would concentrate on what was happening now. Strangers were taking control of her life and she couldn't let that happen. She'd learned the hard way that the only person you could really count on was yourself. First step — stay in control.

Where the hell are they taking me anyway?

This is crap! She needed answers and now. She leaned forward and shook Daniel's shoulder.

Daniel jerked his head around. He handed her a headset and waited while she put it on. "Everything all right? Is there a problem?"

"Yes, there's a problem. And I'm not all right. I need to know where you're taking me and when I can go home."

He smiled at her. A sexy, lopsided smile, and she forgot to breathe.

"Trust me. Everything's going to be okay."

She smiled back weakly. What else could she do? Her chest felt like hundreds of butterflies were swarming around her heart. *That smile should be illegal.* All he had to do was flash those pearly whites and make that dimple appear and she was a goner.

If she didn't stop herself, she could fall hard for this guy. Not only was he the best-looking man she'd ever seen in her life, but he seemed really nice. And those sexy eyes and the killer smile... *Whoa, baby!* She instinctively felt she could trust him, but could she trust herself?

* * * *

"We lost her," said the silver-haired man.

His colleague on the other end of the telephone cursed. "What do you mean you lost her? How could that have happened?"

"She disappeared off the train, but she can't get far on that injured leg."

"You must find her. She can't be allowed to destroy all we've achieved. We've come too far. I want her eliminated."

"Of course... I'll take care of it."

The silver-haired man replaced the phone in its cradle and swore. He smashed his fist on his desk and stormed out of the room, slamming the door behind him. He didn't want to do it, but this time he had no choice.

It was time to call in all favors.

* * * *

The helicopter circled around a small cabin in a clearing, the surrounding area appeared to be miles of dense bushland. As they hovered and began their descent, Daniel removed his headset and seatbelt, then moved to the rear compartment. He jumped out of the door as soon as the pilot opened it and reached for Beth's hand to help her out. She brushed him aside and leaped out on her own steam. She'd had enough heat for the time being, thank you very much.

Daniel shrugged and reached into the cockpit to grab her backpack. The pilot climbed back in the helicopter after throwing a few extra bags on the ground and gave Daniel the thumbs-up sign before taking off and flying into the distance.

"We'd better get inside," Daniel said, as soon as the helicopter was out of sight. "Here, take my arm," he offered.

"I can manage."

"Suit yourself," Daniel answered, chuckling softly as he led the way to the small cabin ahead.

Beth hurried to catch up with him, limping heavily and cursing herself for refusing his help. She just couldn't let him get close to her. If she leaned on him now for support, knowing how the slightest physical contact affected her, she wouldn't be able to regain the control she so desperately needed.

Beth stopped for a minute to rest her leg and inspect the cabin. Larger than she'd first thought, it had bare timber walls and louvre shutters that gave the impression of age, however the gabled roof was a jungle-green corrugated iron, which hinted of recent renovations. Several timber steps led to a small veranda across the front of the building. The front door was open and Daniel leaned against the doorframe, grinning down at her, his brown eyes twinkling in amusement.

"Are you sure you don't want any help, Miss Hamilton? I don't bite, you know."

Beth flushed at his words, once more reminded that he was absolutely gorgeous. Her heart pounded away so loudly that she was sure he could hear it.

"Nn-n-no thanks," she stammered. "I'm good, almost there." She started forward but caught her foot on a tree root and stumbled. She felt her legs crumple under her as she fell unceremoniously to the ground.

Daniel reached her in seconds, enfolding her in his strong arms and lifting her upright. She instinctively pulled away from him and he stepped back, leaving his hands resting on her upper arms, branding her.

"Easy now, it's not a crime to accept help, you know."

Beth trembled as the tears that had been threatening all day finally came out in a deluge. "I'm s-sorry." She bowed her head and raised a hand to wipe her eyes. The last thing she needed was for him to see her crying.

Daniel stifled a curse and drew her to his chest. She felt her body sink into him as he gently rubbed her back before easing her head to rest against his shoulder.

"It's going to be all right. You're safe now," he whispered.

The kind words of comfort intended to calm her unleashed a floodgate. Beth cried as she'd never cried before. All the pain and anguish of the last eight weeks — the operation, the memory loss, the nightmares — all collided with her thoughts and emotions, and combined with today's horrifying events, came out in a torrent of tears. She leaned her body into his. He didn't push her away. He just held on. The warmth of his arms and the tenderness of his touch made her feel safe and protected. It was difficult to move out of that comfort zone, but after several minutes when the sobs began to die down, Daniel drew back.

"Let's get inside and have something to eat," he said. "I don't know about you, but I'm starved."

The tears had released much of the tension she'd been feeling ever since that day she'd woken up in hospital, but that didn't change the fact that she'd just made an idiot of herself in front of a total stranger. A drop-dead gorgeous stranger who was apparently in charge of her life for the time being. *Way to go, Beth.*

Beth leaned heavily on Daniel's arm as she made her way into the cabin. He held her firmly, but gently, as she hobbled over to a shabby but comfy-looking couch, and suggested she put her leg up while he prepared some food. Beth glanced at her watch and realized it was only lunchtime. Three hours ago she had boarded a train, hoping to get some answers, and now, here she was in a remote cabin with a stranger and more questions than she'd started with. She slumped back against the comfortable cushions and sighed. What the hell was next?

The scent of sausages and bacon filled the air as Daniel returned from the kitchenette on the other side of the large living room. "You want some coffee?"

"I'd kill for a cup of coffee," Beth replied, trying to sound cheerful. "And that food smells fantastic. I really am hungry."

Daniel placed a tray on the coffee table in front of Beth. The sausages and bacon were delicious and the coffee went a long way to warm the chill Beth had felt ever since that moment in the train when she had started to remember. He also handed Beth a glass of water and a couple of pain pills for her leg, which she gratefully took.

"You seem to have everything here, food, coffee, pills... What is this place?" Beth asked.

"It's a safe house. We keep it fairly well stocked with vacuum-packed frozen meat and tinned food. You never know when it might be needed," he replied, as he sat down in the armchair opposite her.

"We, meaning the NCA?"

"Yes."

"So why is the National Crimes Agency interested in my train crash? And where do I fit in with all this?"

Daniel paused briefly before replying. "We're not completely sure, but we do know it involves national — and possibly international — security. Why don't we finish our meal first, then we'll talk. Okay?"

"And you'll tell me everything?"

"As much as I can," Daniel replied. She was sharp as a tack and as prickly as a pear. He needed to be careful. He couldn't tell her everything, for her own safety, but he knew she wouldn't be satisfied with that.

"I don't know all the facts, but I promise you I'll tell you what I can. Okay?"

Daniel watched Beth, realizing what an effort this conversation was for her. She was really trying to get herself together, but her knee was obviously bothering her. She must be exhausted. He couldn't add to her stress by telling her too much, regardless of how many questions she might have.

He'd only tell her what she needed to know for the moment. Later, when things were more certain, there would be time for the whole truth. He couldn't even tell her how they'd met because he couldn't risk her remembering just yet. If word got out that her memory was back, the people following her would stop at nothing to kill her.

She had to feel the chemistry between them, given her skittishness, but he couldn't afford to do anything except try and ignore it. Realistically he knew he should maintain a professional distance if he was to keep her out of danger and his head straight. He couldn't afford to think of what could happen between them down the track. For now, the present was far more important.

Five minutes later, Beth placed her cup back on the coffee table and sat up, moving her legs off the couch and onto the floor.

"Okay, I'm ready for you to tell me what's going on. I think I deserve that, at least. I've been shot at, thrown off a train and flown to a cabin in the middle of nowhere. You've asked me to trust you and I've done all you asked, so now I'd appreciate an explanation please." Beth leaned forward in her seat. "Whenever you're ready."

Daniel held Beth's gaze for a few more seconds before turning away and rising to his feet. He took a deep breath and blew it our slowly. *Okay, truth time.*

"The train crash wasn't an accident."

"What did you say?" The breath *whooshed* out of Beth's lungs as she fell against the couch.

Daniel reached over and touched her hand. "Let me finish what I have to tell you, then you can ask questions. We're also pretty sure you may have seen something—or someone—on the train that was connected to the crash."

"Why would you think that?" She had been thinking the same thing herself, but she'd hoped that it had just been her overactive imagination. It *was* an explanation for the nightmares she had been having. But what made them think she'd seen anything? Could they possibly know about the nightmares? There was one way…

"Have you been talking to my psychiatrist?" she asked.

"No, should we have?"

That was a relief. "No…but you knew about my memory loss. I just thought you might have discussed it with her."

"Your conversations with your doctor are private. She wouldn't tell us anything, even if we'd asked. Was there something you didn't tell the police about the crash?"

"No. I told them everything I remember…but I still want to know why you think the crash wasn't an accident, and why I'm involved?"

Daniel paused. He appeared to be inwardly debating how he would continue. Beth wondered now just how much of the truth he would tell her, but nothing prepared her for the next words that came out of his mouth.

"The driver didn't have a heart attack. He was shot."

Chapter Three

"He was shot?" Beth nearly jumped off the couch. "Do you think I saw the shooting?"

Daniel's face was a mask. *He'd better tell me the whole truth.*

"We don't know exactly what you saw, but while you were in the hospital, there were some unusual inquiries about you. People who didn't leave names. We also have reason to believe someone may have been following you since you've been back in Sydney."

"You were following me, remember? Did you see someone else?" She was becoming more frightened by the minute. Her heart slammed in her chest and a loud thrumming started inside her head. The nightmares were becoming reality. *What have I got myself into?*

Daniel's eyes filled with remorse as he sat down next to her on the couch. "The most important thing for now is to keep you safe."

"How long do I have to stay here?" Beth asked.

"It shouldn't be longer than a few days, maybe a week."

"A week?" Beth gasped.

"I'm sorry, but we have no choice."

Stunned, Beth slumped back on the couch. She felt so helpless. Her life was spiraling out of control and she didn't know why or how she could stop it, but she resigned herself to do as he asked. She didn't have a choice. She didn't even know where she was, for crying out loud. Her leg wasn't completely healed as yet, so how was she ever going to keep safe by herself? She felt deep in her heart she could trust him. She just hoped to God that her gut feeling was right.

* * * *

The warm water soothed the pain in Beth's leg as she showered in the cabin's bathroom. So many thoughts ran through her head. Despite her earlier feelings, she'd called Dr. Bennett and left a message on his voicemail, letting him know she'd decided to stay for a few extra days. He had a habit of calling in on her, and this should satisfy him for the moment without giving too much away. She certainly hoped so, because if the people after her went to him for information, he couldn't tell them any details. At least she'd explained her absence so he wouldn't think of searching for her. He would be safe for now.

She dried herself off and dressed in a toweling robe before exploring the bedroom. On the double bed lay an old-fashioned patchwork quilt. Timber shutters covered the window and as she drew closer she saw metal bars between the glass and the wood. The cupboard was painted white and matched the small chest of drawers beside the bed. Someone must have spent a lot of time flicking through the Ikea catalogue.

Inside the cupboard Beth found a selection of clothing. Daniel had told her to help herself to anything that fit, as the clothes were there to be used by the occupants of this safe house. She chose a plain cotton nightdress and flung it on the bed. A soft knock on the door made her jump. She drew the sides of the bathrobe closer together.

"Come in."

Daniel opened the door and walked inside, his large frame making the room appear smaller. "I thought you might like some hot chocolate to help you sleep." He stepped farther inside and placed a steaming mug on the bedside table.

"Thank you."

Daniel had also showered and was now dressed in jeans and a white T-shirt that stretched across his muscled chest. Beth had difficulty stopping herself from staring below his eye level, but she really should stop doing it. She hated it when guys did that to her. *Oh baby!* Flushing, she turned away.

"Well, if that was all you wanted, I think I'll turn in now," Beth rasped. "Thanks for the hot chocolate."

"Beth?" Daniel asked. He grabbed her hand. "Are you okay? Do you need anything else?"

Her mouth went dry and she licked her lips unconsciously as she fought to control her feelings.

It's just lust, remember. Get over it. He's not really moving in for a kiss.

He seemed to be staring at her mouth and moving closer.

"No, I'm fine," she lied, as she pulled away from him. He didn't resist.

"I've got my pain tablets here with me. Thanks again for the hot chocolate," she said, stepping backward and trying to sound natural.

Daniel turned to leave. "Sleep well," he said as he walked away. "Call me if you need anything."

"Sure," she answered. She heard Daniel curse as he walked away from her door. She exhaled when she heard the door to his room close softly. She lay on her bed, thinking. What would have happened if she hadn't taken fright? He wanted to kiss her, and if she was truthful with herself, *she* wanted *him* to kiss her. She could still feel the heat from the nearness of his body. She was crazy.

This sucks.

She was so totally out of her depth here, and judging by that curse outside her door, he wasn't too happy about it either. Heck, someone was trying to kill her and all she could think about was jumping his bones. *Am I weird or what?*

Beth was asleep as soon as her head hit the pillow, however, minutes later she woke to find a figure standing beside her bed. She opened her mouth to call for help but a hand covered her mouth.

"It's only me," whispered Daniel. "Someone's trying to get in. We've got to get out of here right away."

Not again. Beth pulled the covers up to her neck in a protective gesture. "Do I have time to get dressed first?"

"You have one minute, then we're out of here." Daniel turned his back and began throwing small articles into Beth's backpack.

"What are you doing?" she asked.

"You're going to need the pain pills and a change of clothes. Hurry up. We've got to leave."

With no time to worry about modesty, Beth finished pulling on the jeans and jumper she'd left out before going to bed. She slipped on the jogging shoes she'd found in the cupboard, then grabbed a coat before joining Daniel at the door.

"I think they're inside. We'd better go out the window. Think you can handle it?"

"Hey, I made it off the train, didn't I?"

"Okay," Daniel said, as he inserted a strange-looking key into a slot at the edge of the frame and opened the entire window, including the bars. "I'll help you out. Wait for me."

After Daniel had lifted her through the opening, she crouched close to the house while he followed her out, closing the window silently after him. He led the way to the rear of the cabin and headed toward a wall of shrubbery. A clicking noise sounded and Beth was amazed to see a large garage door open—behind it, a black Range Rover.

"Get in," Daniel urged. She didn't need any encouragement as she jumped into the passenger seat and slammed the door. Daniel roared the engine into life, spinning the wheels and driving off at high speed down the track. Two men ran out of the cabin. The last thing Beth heard as they sped off was the explosive sound of bullets shattering the passenger side mirror as the shots unsuccessfully sought their target.

* * * *

The journey down the rough bush track was anything but smooth. The frequent rain in the area had forged deep trenches and even though Daniel valiantly tried driving around them, at the speed they were traveling that was nearly impossible. After half an hour of speeding, Daniel slowed down to a crawl and turned briefly to check on Beth. Her face was pinched and her eyes were shuttered. What must she be thinking about all of this? He certainly didn't know what to make of it.

One thing he did know was that it shouldn't have happened. There must've been a leak in the department. No one else had known where they were. *But who could it be?* Daniel knew these people and couldn't imagine anyone selling them out. As he negotiated the difficult track, he came to a decision. He needed Beth's help to get through this, and as soon as they found another place to hide, he'd tell her the whole story. In the meantime, they needed to work together.

A few minutes later, Daniel checked their position and keyed more information into the GPS.

"How did they find us?" asked Beth. He could tell she was trying to keep calm, but the thought that she'd been found at the cabin where she was supposed to be safe must be terrifying for her. It scared the shit out of him.

"I have my suspicions, but I can't be sure. For now, we need to get as far away from here as we can."

"So where are we going then?"

Daniel continued driving while he answered her, "We're going to a remote campsite I know. I used to go camping there with my father when I was younger. No one knows about it, as far as I know. We should be safe there for the time being."

"You're kidding, right? Camping. I *hate* camping. My dad always used to say that staying in a cheap motel was the only camping he would ever do, and I agree with him."

He smiled. "I'm sure you'll survive for one night. We can't risk staying in another safe house, and a motel is out of the question. They'd find us for sure." He knew it must be tough on her, but so far she was holding up better than he expected. A few grumbles about the conditions wasn't much to put up with. Let her have her gripes if it made her feel better. *God, she has guts*, he thought. She'd followed all his instructions without question, but she had to be hurting. Hopefully when they got to the campsite, he could make some calls and find out what the fuck happened.

* * * *

The sun started to rise above the dense bushland as they pulled into a clearing. Tall gum trees surrounded the area with several fallen branches strewn around. In the center of the clearing was a pile of charred logs, indicating a previous campfire. The *whooshing* sound of running water was heard as soon as Daniel turned off the car. He jumped out and moved to the passenger door to help Beth. She started to protest but Daniel cut her off. "We've been through this before, haven't we?"

Beth flushed but forced herself to look at him. "I'm sorry. I'm just not used to people helping me. I've had to fend for myself for a long time. I'm not very good at accepting help." He nodded and held out his hand. She reached over to take it when he surprised her and placed both his arms around her, quickly lifting her out of the vehicle, carrying her across to the edge of the clearing and gently placing her onto a fallen log that remarkably resembled a stool.

"Now that wasn't so bad, was it?" Daniel chuckled as he saw her surprised expression. "You'll have to get used to it because until your leg is healed and we catch whoever is after you, you're going to need my help."

Not giving Beth a chance to reply, Daniel walked away and started unpacking the four-wheel drive. Out came an assortment of camping gear — a dome tent, blow-up mattresses, sleeping bags, even a small gas stove. A box filled with tinned food and a kettle appeared. He quickly cleared a flattened area of dirt and erected the tent. He took the kettle and disappeared in the direction of the running water and returned a few minutes later to place it on the lighted stove. Beth watched him while he worked. He walked with confidence and purpose. His broad shoulders and well-defined arms showed through the tight T-shirt, his muscular legs giving the impression of strength and power as he strode over and sat on the ground in front of her. Heat was still permeating her skin from where he had touched her when he'd lifted her from the Range Rover. Now that he'd shifted closer to her, she could hear her heart pounding and her breathing became shallow.

Stop it. He was staring at her with one of those devastating smiles again, and she was lost in a dream of forbidden pleasures, picturing his beautiful mouth and strong hands doing extraordinary things to her naked body.

"Earth to Beth."

"I'm sorry. Did you say something?" Beth glanced at Daniel, feeling the heat seep up to her neck and over her face. She'd been too busy getting hot and bothered to hear what Daniel had been saying. *This has got to stop.*

Daniel smiled at her, a glint of humor in his eyes. "I asked if you wanted anything to eat with the coffee. It's been some time since we last ate, and since we're stuck here for a while, we might as well get some sustenance."

"Yes, I suppose so. How long will we be here?" she asked.

"Probably until tomorrow morning. I have to make some calls first. We should know more after I finish, but for the moment, we rest."

Beth watched Daniel as he poured the coffee. He had this amazing effect on her and she had no idea how she was going to get through this situation if she didn't cool down. Maybe if she tried to think of something else. Something safe and boring. Diversionary tactics, that's what her mother had told her to do when she had to do something she didn't like. *Think of something completely different to take my mind off it.* Beth smiled to herself. She could always think of the dentist every time he came near her. She hated the dentist. Maybe that would do it.

Nah, that won't work. It was going to be a long day.

* * * *

Daniel watched Beth, studying her face as she looked into the distance. She was so beautiful sitting there on that log, her magnificent red hair blowing in wisps across her face in time to the breeze. She must have had a lot of questions, but so far she'd shown considerable restraint in pursuing any answers. He wondered what she was thinking and was a little bit in awe of her trust in him. She had to be frightened to death and confused in the bargain, but she displayed more courage than any woman he'd ever met. She deserved to be told the truth, but he couldn't bring himself to get into that just yet. He'd rather enjoy the moment here in these peaceful surroundings with a beautiful woman for company. It wouldn't be long before he had to get them on the road again.

He retrieved the satellite phone from the car. Now was probably a good time to make a few calls, because he couldn't make any decisions until he had more information. They were safe here for the moment since no one else knew about this place except perhaps his father, and he knew his father wouldn't be contacted. He hadn't spoken to him in five years and the people he worked for knew that.

Beth was the only loose end, as far as the bad guys were concerned. Damn, he wished they'd just placed her under protection in the first place, but his boss had thought it better to watch her from a distance, given her memory loss. They didn't even know if what she remembered would be useful. What they needed was an

ID on the assassin. But it didn't seem to matter anymore if she remembered or not. The bastards were trying to kill her anyway. He couldn't let that happen.

Although he hadn't seen the face of the gunman, Daniel had recognized the man who'd been shot. He'd never met him but had seen him before at government functions. Peter Wilson had been a senior public servant in the Foreign Affairs department. He'd been responsible for the schedule of events for the British Prime Minister at the upcoming Commonwealth Heads of Government Conference to be held in Brisbane next week.

After his death they'd found that large sums of money had been deposited into a bank account in his name. The indications were that Wilson had sold confidential details to some unknown party — possibly a terrorist organization or an unfriendly foreign government.

If this scenario was true, then Beth wasn't the only target. If someone had leaked their location, they probably knew Daniel had been on the train and was with her now. But other than himself, only three people knew he'd been there and that Beth had seen the face of the gunman. Beth, his boss and Will, the helicopter pilot who'd flown them to the cabin. He'd stake his life that none of them would betray him. It had to be someone else, but he couldn't risk calling just anyone in the department. There was only a couple of people he could trust.

Once again glancing at Beth, Daniel realized he couldn't put it off any longer. If he wanted her to help herself and cooperate fully with him, he had to tell her the whole story. Striding toward her more confidently than he felt, he saw Beth turn her head sharply toward him, an expectant expression greeting him as he reached the tree stump and sat.

"You're ready to tell me what you neglected to say before?"

Of course she'd figured out he'd been holding back. Her patience with him today had been remarkable. Anyone else would have been screaming at him to explain hours before this, but Beth somehow seemed to understand that he would tell her in his own time.

Daniel took a deep breath, then blew it out slowly. "You're sure you're ready for this?" he asked.

"I'm not sure I want to know, but I'm positive I need to."

"Okay then, this is the information I have."

He left nothing out, including how they'd met and how she'd seen the shooting on the train. He saw a myriad of emotions flicker over her face as he spoke. Surprise gave way to horror and fear, only to be replaced by a seething anger as she realized the full impact of what he had just told her.

"I'm sorry I couldn't tell you this all before. We thought it would protect you if you didn't know. I know you must be angry."

"Angry doesn't even begin to describe how I'm feeling right now," said Beth, her voice quiet, but formal and controlled. She clutched her walking stick for dear life as she struggled to stand.

"My leg is really stiff," she said, as she hobbled off in the direction of the creek. "I think I need a walk to stretch it out."

Knowing better than to offer help, Daniel watched her in admiration as she staggered before straightening up and walking off into the distance, all the while trying valiantly to mask her limp. He was constantly amazed at her strength. Obviously she needed to be by herself to mull over what she had just learned. He'd leave her alone, but not for too long. They needed to talk about what their next step would be. He owed it to her to keep her informed.

Daniel strolled over to the four-wheel drive and removed a large black suitcase. He carried it over to the campsite where he opened it carefully and expertly assembled the equipment. It didn't take him long to have the satellite dish and the laptop set up. Soon he was online and scanning through the NCA site, searching for clues as to who might be behind this breach of security. He also attached a small black box to his phone and turned it on, punching the numbers from memory. The tension built behind his eyes as he stared at the screen, waiting for one of the few people he trusted to answer.

"Addison," the deep voice on the other end of the phone announced.

"John…"

"Wyatt. Where the fuck are you, mate? We checked out the cabin and you'd vanished. What happened?"

"Change of plan—we had visitors."

"Shit. How the fuck did anyone find you? Only Will and I knew you were there."

"Well, someone found out and I'd like to know how."

"So would I. Where are you now?"

"I think it's better if you don't know until we know who the leak is. We'll be safer this way. Any news on the threat?"

"No, nothing concrete. Does she remember anything? It would be useful to show her some mugshots to help identify the assassin."

"*Now* you want to question her? We should have done it before. She could have been protected all this time. I never agreed with this sit-back-and-wait policy of yours, John."

"I had my reasons, Daniel, but they don't apply now that there seems to be a leak. I agree you need to keep your location under wraps for now. Let me do some checking and I'll get back to you tonight."

"No, I'll call you. I've got scramblers in place. I'll get back to you in twenty-four hours."

The phone clicked off and Daniel set it down on the makeshift table, continuing to sift through pages on the computer screen. The phone call had told him nothing he didn't already know. Hopefully John would be able to give him something to go on when he made contact later on. In the meantime there wasn't much he could do but stay put.

As long as no one knew where they were, they were safe. He hoped they stayed that way, but if someone got to them at the safe house, then it was possible they'd be found here, too.

* * * *

Beth's need to know had burned inside her all day. She'd tried not to show Daniel how much it got to her, and it'd just about killed her to sit and wait for him to tell her. She figured if she appeared too emotional, he wouldn't divulge everything. She'd tried hard to make him believe she was strong, even though the opposite was closer to the truth. Now she almost wished he hadn't said anything.

Her breathing was fast and ragged as she once again turned away from Daniel and hobbled into the bushland. She'd figured out over the last day that someone wanted her dead, but the complexity of the situation was much more than she could ever have imagined.

Why hadn't the police told her all this from the start? Why let her think she was going crazy? And she *had* thought she was going mad. She'd really wondered at the state of her mind and hated feeling that loss of control. It was suddenly too much to take in at once. What the hell was she going to do now? She couldn't think—didn't *want* to think, so she did the thing she always did when things got to be overwhelming. She took a deep breath and centered herself, concentrating on her surroundings and letting her muscles relax. After a session of meditation, she'd always felt better able to cope with anything. She hoped it worked this time.

The late morning sun was hot as it rested on Beth's head. She sat at the side of the creek, feet dangling in the cool water. A pair of rainbow lorikeets rummaged through the undergrowth on the other side of the creek, foraging for food. Beth smiled wistfully as she watched them take turns bringing small tidbits up to their nest in the tall branches of the ghost gum tree. She remembered learning at school that lorikeets mate for life, just like her parents had. She blinked back tears as she thought of them. She missed them so much. She needed them now like never before.

Wiping her eyes, she continued watching the birds. As a child she'd dreamed of having that kind of simplicity in her own life. She wanted to be a part of a loving couple, both sharing the task of bringing up a family. But since her parents had died, she didn't trust relationships. People don't always stick around.

After learning of the danger she was in, she doubted if a relationship was ever going to be possible for her now, even if she'd wanted it. Her head throbbed and she placed her fingers to her temples, gently rubbing to stave off the headache that was lingering below the surface.

The Heads of Government Conference was starting in a few days. Daniel had told her that the security had been tightened and they were aware of the danger, so perhaps after the Conference was over they would be safe? It was a faint hope she was holding on to — wishing with all her heart that there was an end in sight. She had to wait it out and rely on Daniel, even though she hated being dependent on others.

The distant sound of an airplane startled Beth and brought her attention back to her surroundings. She watched the familiar shape of the aircraft float by as she tied her shoelaces, wincing at the dull ache in her leg. She waited for the pain to subside before scrambling to her feet and making her way back to the campsite. She badly needed a nap. She was so tired that she couldn't think straight. Maybe after a rest, she'd be strong enough to deal with the next phase of her life. There wasn't much else to do anyway. Sitting around fantasizing about Daniel would accomplish nothing except build frustration and make things more difficult in the long run.

* * * *

Dinner was uncomfortably silent as both of them went through the motions of eating the tinned meat from the rations. Daniel searched Beth's face, trying but failing to gauge what she was thinking. Her face was tight and expressionless, as she seemed to be keeping a tight grip on her emotions. That was probably good, he thought. She needed to be in control until they got out of this mess.

Despite the nap she'd taken that afternoon, they both needed to get a good night's sleep. Last night had certainly been a write-off in that department. God only knew when they might get another chance for a rest. Tomorrow was shaping up to be another long day.

Beth finished eating quickly and made them both some coffee. Daniel watched as she maneuvered her injured leg about the campsite and over to the stove. Her independence amused him, but he also admired her for it. Most people would have fallen in a heap with only half of what had happened to her in the last twenty-four hours, but she'd managed to keep it all together and keep going. She was going to need all of that strength and more before this was over.

Dusk settled in and the temperature dropped dramatically. As the birds settled in their nests for the night, the daytime sounds of the bush diminished and were replaced by the creaking of cicadas and the whisper of a breeze through the trees.

"We should get some sleep. We need to get moving again in the morning, and I'd like to get an early start," Daniel said as he finished packing away the plates.

Beth placed a mug of coffee on the log beside Daniel and reached out to touch his arm. "Where will we go?"

He laid his hand gently on top of hers, wanting to prolong the current of electricity trailing across his skin. "I'm not sure yet. I have another call to make in the morning then I'll let you know. In the meantime, get some rest." He wasn't ready to move his hand just yet, leaving it to linger on the softness of her warm skin.

He felt rather than heard Beth's soft intake of breath before she cleared her throat and coughed. "There's only one tent," she rasped.

He shook his head. "You take it."

Shrugging in annoyance, she pulled her arm away and moved back to sit on the log nearer the tent. "Don't be ridiculous. We'd better share it. You'll freeze out here with no fire."

"I'll live. I've done it before." He stifled a smile as he saw her flustered face.

"And you call me stubborn." She stood and threw the almost full mug of coffee onto the dirt behind her. "Okay—but if you get cold later, don't blame me."

Beth grabbed her backpack from beside her and walked off, making her way to the tent. It was sheltered under a tree at the edge of the clearing. She tugged at the zipper but it wouldn't budge.

What now?

She tried once more, but still no luck.

Shit.

Once again she had to ask Daniel for help, and that grated. It was only a little thing, hardly worth worrying about really, she told herself. But it still grated.

She glanced back to where she'd left Daniel. He was watching her. Grinning. *Oh Hell.* He was enjoying this.

"Are you going to just stand there like a stuffed dummy, or are you going to help me?"

"Sorry, I know how you hate to accept help. I thought I'd wait until I was asked. Wouldn't want to be accused of taking over and all."

"Well...I'm asking."

"Asking for what?"

"Oh, for crying out loud... Can you help me with this zipper...please?"

"Now that wasn't so hard, was it?"

Beth gave him her best withering glare. One that would've shrunk most men, but Daniel wasn't most men. He laughed and strode over to her. With one quick flick of his wrist he had the tent open.

"Thanks."

Daniel started to reply, but Beth didn't give him a chance. She quickly threw herself inside the tent and shut the flap before he had a chance to open his mouth. She heard a chuckle as he walked away. She lay back onto the air mattress and relaxed. She glanced at the tent flap and laughed. At least he had a sense of humor.

She shouldn't have been so uptight with him but she couldn't help herself. There was a tension between them she couldn't explain, but now wasn't the time to explore it.

Despite the rough conditions, it didn't take Beth long to fall asleep. She was exhausted, not just physically, but emotionally. Perhaps it was a combination of that plus the painkillers, but moments after she'd crept into her sleeping bag, she was asleep and dreaming once more.

A dark, shadowy figure was moving toward her. She was running, fearing for her life. The bush track became narrower, and she came to a dead end. She turned her head from side to side, her breathing labored. There was no escape.

She turned to the track to find the figure had now reached her. The man wore a mask and was holding a gun pointed directly at her. She gasped as he removed his mask and smiled malevolently at her. His face. As he started to talk, she realized there was something familiar about his face. "You won't get away this time, Miss Hamilton!"

"You! What do you want from me?"

He ignored her question and cocked the trigger of his gun. Beth screamed.

"No!"

Chapter Four

"Beth—wake up!"

"No! No—don't shoot me!" she shouted as she continued her battle with an unseen opponent.

"Beth, it's only a dream. It's me, Daniel."

"Daniel?" Beth stopped struggling and opened her eyes. Daniel gazed at her with concern.

"You okay?"

"Yes, I think so."

Beth dragged herself up onto her elbows. It was still dark except for the light from Daniel's flashlight. There was a pungent smell of burning wood in the air. "Is that smoke I'm smelling?"

"It's a bush fire. Not too close at the moment, but the wind has picked up so that could change at any minute."

"Shit, we've got to move again."

"My thoughts exactly. I've packed most of the equipment already. If you're up to packing your things, we should be ready to roll in about ten minutes."

"Of course I'm up to it. I'll see you in five."

Exactly five minutes later, Beth had changed clothes, packed her knapsack and started dismantling the tent.

Daniel watched her from his position by the car. Grinning, he checked his watch and flashed a smile at Beth before walking back to her.

"I'll do that. You go get in the car."

She nodded then made her way to the Range Rover. Her leg was throbbing, but it was moving more freely now. With all the excitement of the last day, she'd had little time to think about it. She hadn't used her walking stick since before dinner and it felt better to be moving unencumbered. She smiled to herself. At least something was working out.

Daniel packed the last of the gear and closed the tailgate. He threw a couple of blankets into the back seat and placed several water canteens on top of them. The smoke was getting thicker now and the acrid smell burned Beth's nostrils. They needed to hurry. Daniel started up the four-wheel drive and drove down the track.

The black clouds of smoke grew thicker overhead as they drove, masking the dawn. The sky was dark, but not like anything Beth had ever seen before. The temperature was rising—she could feel the burning heat inside the car. The air seemed thick with texture and form. Frightened animals raced along the side of the track, fleeing the flames. The smell of burning eucalypts was almost overpowering. Beth covered her mouth and nose with her hands, but it had little effect. Her throat was closing up as the wheezing took over.

Daniel turned off the air conditioning and closed the air vents.

"Grab those towels from the back and soak them in water. We can wrap them around our faces. It should help with the smoke."

Beth nodded. Talking was impossible as she coughed the irritating smoke from her throat. Daniel slowed the car down as she helped him to tie a damp towel around his nose and mouth.

A wall of red-hot flames and black smoke rose to the left as Beth peered out of the window. The wind had picked up and driven the fire toward them.

"Daniel!"

Daniel turned his head at her cry. The flames reached at least three stories high and were heading straight for them. His reaction was instantaneous.

"Bloody hell! We have to find some shelter quickly. Watch on the right for any large rocks or ravines we can shelter behind."

Beth skimmed the landscape anxiously. It was difficult to see anything with the thick smoke masking the terrain. Suddenly, a large rock jutted out through the smoky haze.

"Over there…a large rock and it has some sort of a cave under it."

Daniel didn't waste any time, driving quickly over the rough ground and under the rocky outcrop. Beth silently thanked Daniel's supervisors for the four-wheel drive vehicle.

The fire rushed forward with incredible speed. Beth held her breath as the stifling heat inside the car burned her nose and throat. Daniel reached into the back and grabbed the water bottles and blankets he'd thrown in before they'd left the campsite.

"Here…take these," he said as he threw her one of each. "I'll jump in the back. Lie down and cover yourself with the blanket. We should be safe if we stay down. Drink plenty of the water. I'll let you know when it's safe to get up."

"How long do you think it'll be?" Beth asked anxiously.

"Firestorms move through pretty quickly," said Daniel as he gave her one of those heart-stopping smiles to reassure her. "It shouldn't be long. We'll be okay."

The roar was deafening as the fire swept closer. It was like being in the center of an explosion. Beth dragged the blanket over herself as she lay across the front seats. Covering her ears to block out the noise, she thought about how her life was turning into one disaster after another. Beads of sweat dripped from her face onto the seat below her. The intensity of the heat was like nothing she had ever experienced before. Surprisingly, she wasn't as fearful as she'd expected. Sure, she was scared, but somehow Daniel's cool confidence gave her strength. Thank God he was here with her.

Time seemed to stand still as the roar of the fire receded. Beth ran her tongue over her cracked lips. She coughed as the pungent smell of the flames gripped her throat. Taking a long drink from the water bottle, she listened for sounds of what might be happening outside. She checked her watch and realized it had been almost an hour since they'd left the campsite and at least half an hour since the firestorm had passed over. She moved the blanket away from her head and sat up.

The scene outside the car window resembled the aftermath of a nuclear holocaust. The previously lush greenery was blackened and small spires of smoke rose sporadically over the landscape. Tree trunks, which only moments before had held branches thick with foliage, were now stark columns. The air remained thick with smoke, but visibility was improving as the fire continued on its forward path and away from their position.

Beth touched the window tentatively to test the heat. She jerked her hand away as the glass burned. Turning around, she saw Daniel sit up and scan the area. She slid through the gap in the seats, sitting next to him in the back. His face was drawn tight and his eyes crinkled at the edges where he squinted. She had a sudden urge to touch him, soothe his worry lines and smooth his brow.

"Are you okay?" he asked huskily as she removed the wet cloth from around his neck and wiped his sweat-beaded forehead.

"I think so," Beth answered, continuing to tentatively wipe the cool cloth over his heated face. "How long before we can get out of the car?"

He grabbed her wrist, stalling her progress and searing her skin. The heat in his eyes had nothing to do with the temperature outside and everything to do with their mutual need. Her breath hitched as she waited for his next move.

As he answered, his eyes never left hers and the tension inside the car cranked up several notches. "The ground will still be extremely hot for a while yet. I'll check on it in another half an hour. I'm more worried about the equipment and the car. If any of that was damaged, we'll be stuck here for some time."

He took hold of the cloth as he released her hand. Beth gasped when he reciprocated, wiping the cloth over her cheeks and down to her neck. "Won't the firefighters find us?" she asked.

Daniel shook his head while he continued to slide the cloth downward, reaching into the opening of her shirt before pulling his hand out and throwing the cloth onto the seat beside her. *Damn.* Maybe he was right to stop, but her body didn't want him to.

"Beth...this is the center of a national park. The firefighters will be concentrating their efforts around the edge of the park, near the townships. I'm afraid they'll probably just let this fire burn itself out."

Beth turned her face away, her eyes watering and her heart turning somersaults. She forced a couple of slow breaths in and out. "So what's next then?"

"Pray for rain?" *Bloody hell, what am I doing?* He'd nearly ripped her shirt off and tasted her there and then. And she might very well have let him. He shifted in place as his jeans tightened over his thickening groin. *Down boy—just a job, remember? No attachments, no problems, keep focused.*

A muffled buzzing sound filled the car. Turning his head from side to side, Daniel tried to get a fix on where it was coming from.

"What's that noise?"

"I'm not sure."

"It sounds like it's coming from the back of the car."

The back of the car? It had to be the satellite phone. It must have survived the heat. This was good news.

Daniel reached over the back seat and found the source of the buzzing. He attached a small box, pressed the receive button and raised the phone to his ear. A harried voice started talking immediately, not waiting for Daniel to reply.

"Wyatt! Where in blazes have you been? I've been worried shitless. When you didn't call at the arranged time, I decided I'd better call you."

"Addison...we're okay. Just a little delay, that's all. Sorry I didn't make the call on time."

Beth tilted her head to the side and opened her mouth to speak. Daniel shrugged and put up his hand to stop her from talking. He didn't know who he could trust at this stage and he felt it would be better to keep details to a minimum. There was a leak and he didn't want to take any chances.

"Delay? Anything I should know about?"

"Everything's under control for now. Have you learned anything on your end?"

"Nothing yet. I've swept my office and my home for bugs. Will's done the same. So far nothing has shown up. Will is checking the security videos as we speak. I thought it best not to involve anyone else for the moment."

Daniel closed his eyes and rubbed his temple with his free hand. He hesitated briefly before replying. "I agree. The fewer personnel involved the better. We have to find out who the leak is as soon as possible. Not only is the security of the Conference in jeopardy, but Beth Hamilton's life is in danger as well."

"Yours, too, Daniel. You have to be very careful. What's your position at the moment? Do I need to send Will in to get you?"

Staring out of the window and over the burned landscape, Daniel took a deep breath, letting it out slowly. "No, we're fine for the moment. We're moving to a new location. I'll call you in a few hours." Daniel cut the connection before his boss had a chance to reply. No explanations meant less chance of them being found again.

As soon as Daniel replaced the phone, Beth leaned forward slightly and touched Daniel's hand. "Why didn't you tell your boss what happened? Do you think he's the leak?"

Daniel stared at the place where her skin touched his before turning away. "Of course not. My boss is the one person I do trust, but the only way I can see to keep us safe is to tell no one where we are—and that includes my boss. It's the only way to plug up the leak."

Beth picked up the wet cloth she'd used on Daniel's face and folded it neatly before placing it back on the seat between them. "What about the Conference? If someone knows about us, then what about the security team? They need to know the arrangements have changed."

"Yes, I thought of that." He sighed as he blew out a breath. "We need to get out of here and find the leak before it's too late."

She stared at Daniel, her voice almost a whisper, "How long do we have?"

He straightened in his seat. "The Conference starts next Tuesday."

"That's only five days away," she gasped, clenching her fists as they lay on her lap.

"That's why we need to get out of here—the sooner the better."

* * * *

Silence descended as they waited impatiently for their surroundings to cool down enough to move on. Daniel checked the electronic equipment and found it all to be in working order. The GPS had pinpointed their position and Daniel worked out a route to get them out of the park. All they waited on now was enough time for a drop in temperature in the petrol tank so the fuel would return to liquid, and the tires would be cool enough to take the weight of the vehicle.

Minutes ticked by and Beth tapped her fingers on the armrest beside her. Sighing, she gingerly touched the window. It was still warm, but bearable.

"Should we check the ground temperature? The window isn't too hot now. Surely the ground would cool down faster than the car?" Beth asked.

"I'd like to wait a little while longer. The tires may still be soft from the heat and I don't want to risk a blowout. Don't worry. It won't be much longer. I promise," Daniel answered as he flashed her a reassuring grin.

There it was again, that killer smile. Beth smiled shyly back. Feeling her cheeks start to burn, she turned her head and stared out her window again. At least this attraction thing was distracting her from being completely terrified by the situation. That had to be a plus, didn't it? Beth knew she should control her lascivious thoughts, but she couldn't help herself, and she was so grateful he was around. She'd be dead now if not for him. Perhaps that was what she was feeling — gratitude. Maybe she was reading too much into this, but then she remembered the burning tingles when she touched his face earlier. And that session with the towel... *Hoo wee, talk about intense heat!* No, this certainly wasn't just gratitude, but she couldn't think about it now. After this was over, she probably wouldn't see him ever again. *Get over it, Beth.*

Beth sighed inwardly and straightened her shoulders. A brilliant flash of light suddenly lit up the sky and a crash of thunder sounded a few seconds later.

A few tentative drops of water fell on the glass before the downpour started. Beth and Daniel smiled at each other.

"Your prayers were answered. Somebody up there likes you, Daniel."

Daniel grinned back at her and winked. "I knew that being an altar boy would come in handy one day. With this rain, we can get moving sooner than we thought.

Let's get out of the car and check the damage before we go."

Daniel and Beth both opened their doors and climbed out of the Rover. The ground felt warm through their shoes and the steadily increasing rain on the ash was making it very slippery. Beth raised her head toward the sky. She closed her eyes as the rain trickled down her face. She knew the water must have left dirty trails through the smoke dust on her cheeks, but she didn't care. It felt too good.

Daniel inspected the engine and refilled the radiator with water. The tires' pressure had dropped but there was still air in them. Enough to drive on if he used the foot pump he had used on the mattresses, Daniel assured her. Beth took a few tentative steps across the ground in front of them, picking up still warm stray branches from their path to clear the way for the vehicle.

Half an hour later, the car started on the third try. Beth breathed a sigh of relief. The rock they had sheltered behind must have been more protective than she'd thought it would be. She'd really thought the car would be history, but luck had been on their side once more. Daniel released the brake, and they were finally on their way.

The thunder and lightning had now abated, but the rain still fell in a steady downpour. The track was developing rivers of its own as Daniel carefully maneuvered the four-wheel drive over the fire-ravaged terrain. Steam rose from the blackened earth as the cooling rain blanketed the ground. The air was clearer now, the smoke slowly dissipating.

* * * *

The journey out of the park was slow and tortured. They were delayed from leaving by local police who questioned their reasons for being in the park. They weren't exactly suspects, but the authorities thought that the fire had been deliberately lit. It took all of Daniel's diplomatic skills and patience to convince the authorities that they were simply a couple who'd been camping and found themselves trapped in a bush fire. Which, in essence, was the truth.

"You handled that well," remarked Beth as they finally found their way to the highway. "I was worried they were going to accuse us of starting the fire."

"I was telling them the truth. We were camping. They didn't need to know why we were there. I usually find if you stick close to the truth, people tend to believe you."

"Do you think it was coincidence that the fire was deliberately lit?" Beth asked.

"It's hard to say. Unfortunately a lot of fires are started on purpose, so there's no reason to think it was anything to do with us. No one knew we were there. Even my boss has no idea where we are. No, I think it's most likely a coincidence," said Daniel. "Right now we have more important things to worry about, like finding somewhere safe to crash while I do some investigating."

"We definitely need to clean up, that's for sure, and I'm just a little bit hungry, too."

Daniel grinned at Beth's attempt to lighten the mood. She managed a slight smile as she gazed back at him.

"Where are we going this time?"

"Canberra. I have a friend who's out of town for a few months and he lets me use his house sometimes. We should be safe enough for tonight, although tomorrow we may need to move again. And we need to get rid of this car. Someone seems to be good at almost finding us, so I don't want to take any chances."

* * * *

It was late afternoon and the sun was low in the sky, shining directly through the windshield, creating a half-light that made visibility difficult. The outer northern suburbs of Canberra were now visible in the distance as they drove smoothly along the Federal Highway. The pit stop they'd made an hour before at the roadhouse in the small township of Wingello had drawn a few curious gazes. It was then Beth had realized they hadn't washed the soot off their faces. After a quick trip to the bathroom for both of them, Daniel had replenished the air in the tires and petrol in the tank, taking the opportunity to clean the windshield and rear window. Thankfully the car was now running more efficiently, not attracting the attention it had when they'd been hobbling along with half-flat tires, even if the paint was peeling away in places. The greasy hot chips and icy cold colas Beth had bought while Daniel was seeing to the car tasted like manna from heaven. But that meal had been a few hours ago and now Beth's stomach rumbled. One thing she could always count on was her stomach. Beth could never be without food for long, even when she was upset. In fact, the more upset she was, the more food she seemed to need. And she needed to eat now. Her stomach started to protest—loudly.

"What was that?"

Oh my God! Did my stomach really make that sound?

"What was what?" Beth countered sheepishly, trying to sound innocent.

Daniel laughed. "I could have sworn I heard a stomach growl." Shaking his head, he turned back toward Beth. "Never mind, we'll be there soon enough. The house is usually stocked with plenty of food."

A short time later they approached the sign for Belconnen and Daniel turned off the highway. They'd driven past Canberra University and turned into a side street next to Lake Ginninderra reserve when Daniel slowed the car down and stopped.

"What's wrong?" Beth whispered.

"I don't know. I just have a bad feeling about this. Jake's house is around the corner and there's a dark blue van parked across the road. I think I'll just cruise past and check it out before we stop."

Daniel leaned over and picked up a couple of baseball caps from the back seat. "Here, put this on," he said as he handed one to Beth and placed the other on his head. Beth rolled her hair into a bun and covered it with the hat. Daniel nodded his approval before he started driving slowly down the street.

"Don't look at the van."

"I'm not entirely without brains, you know."

"Sorry." Daniel's face was drawn and he stared straight ahead, but Beth could see him glancing surreptitiously out of the corner of his eye at the van as they approached. "I was just making sure. We don't want to make them suspicious."

As the car passed the van, Beth let out a breath and whispered softly to Daniel, "What do you think? Are they waiting for us?"

"I'm not sure, but we'll know in a minute." Daniel shifted the car up a gear and planted his foot on the accelerator pedal. The tires shrieked as they took off at high speed down the road. The blue van suddenly came to life and charged after them.

"I think we have our answer," said Daniel. "They're definitely following us."

"Why'd you do that?" Beth shouted. "You said you didn't want to make them suspicious, then you virtually beg them to come and get us."

"I wasn't sure. I didn't recognize the driver, but I had to find out if they were after us." Daniel swore as he swerved to avoid a car coming out of a side street. "Shit! Can we talk about this later? I'm kind of busy right now!"

Chapter Five

Beth clung to her seat as best she could while the car sped precariously through the residential streets of Belconnen. Daniel's face was a mask of sheer concentration as he expertly maneuvered the vehicle away from their pursuers.

"How far away are they now?" asked Daniel.

"About fifty meters, I guess," said Beth, turning around to check through the back window. "We seem to have gained a lead on them."

"Good. There's a shopping center up ahead. We should be able to lose them there if we're lucky."

"I'd better cross all my fingers and toes then."

Daniel smiled wryly. "At least you still have your sense of humor."

"I wasn't joking. We need all the luck we can get."

The shopping center came into view. Daniel entered the car park and slowed down. Dozens of shoppers were driving slowly around the lanes searching for a parking spot.

Everywhere it seemed elderly couples and mothers with children in strollers were negotiating the lanes, making their way to the mall entrance. The blue van followed them into the car park, hovering slowly and checking each lane for signs of their retreat. Daniel saw it creeping up slowly toward them so he waited until another car moved in behind him, then shot out toward the car park exit.

The blue van sped up, but got stuck behind a stream of cars, effectively preventing it from following. The driver blasted the horn, but all that achieved was some rude gestures and shouting from the other drivers. *Too easy.*

Thank God. Beth started to breathe normally again, which was a bit of an effort since she'd been holding her breath for so long. "Where to now?" she asked.

"If we hurry, we can replace the car before the car dealers close then we'll find a place to stay."

"O-kay…so you have an unlimited supply of cash in that duffel bag in the back then?"

"Actually, I do," said Daniel.

Beth turned to him, open-mouthed and wide-eyed, and he chuckled. "Well, almost. I do have enough to get us set up with a different car and to get by for a few days."

An hour later they were driving off from a used car dealer in a rather nondescript white sedan. Daniel even haggled over the price, much to Beth's surprise.

Hoping she could stave off the inevitable growls of hunger, Beth turned to Daniel. "So where's that meal you promised me?"

"Stomach growling again?"

Beth poked her tongue at him. "Enough of the teasing already."

"Thai food okay?" he said as he pulled into the driveway of a five-star hotel.

"I love Thai food, but what are we doing here? Isn't this a little public?"

"Not now," he hushed as the hotel doorman opened the car door for her to get out. "I'll explain later."

Daniel checked them into a suite as Mr. and Mrs. Kelly, a couple from Sydney. Beth felt a flush of heat all over her body at the thought of sharing with him, silently hoping that this 'suite' had more than one room. She'd tried to deny the attraction she felt for him, but geez it was going to be difficult being this close to him.

Stop worrying about it, Beth. Focus on the problem, not the man. Yeah, right!

She needed to get out of this mess. She didn't need a fling with someone she may never see again. Definitely not her style at all. She watched him from behind as he charmed the hotel receptionist while leaning forward on the counter, showing a very sexy rear end. She groaned inwardly. *Oh God.* Focusing on her problems clearly wasn't working. *When this is over, I definitely need to get out more.*

* * * *

As the bellboy opened the room and placed their bags on the stand, Daniel sighed. He was tired from being on the run and he couldn't think straight. Add to that the attraction he felt for Beth and he was worried. Worried that he'd never figure out who was following them. Worried that something bad would happen at the Conference unless he found the leak in the department. Worried that Beth was still in danger. And scared stiff that he wouldn't be able to keep his hands off her.

Without even trying, Beth managed to awaken feelings he had no right to be having. He couldn't afford to have them. This time he wasn't going to get emotionally involved. Emotions got in the way of clear thinking and emotions could get people killed. He couldn't let that happen to anyone again, especially not to Beth. He had to get the job done and fast, and move on.

At least it was a two-room suite. That should give him the space he needed to get some work done. His eyes skimmed the sitting room in front of him. It contained a desk, a three-seater couch, coffee table, a door to the bathroom and a door leading to the bedroom. Next to the desk was a phone plug for Internet connection. He'd take the couch. It was large and at least appeared comfortable.

"I'll take the couch," said Beth, interrupting Daniel's train of thought. "You must be tired from doing all the driving."

"No need. You take the bedroom," Daniel answered. "I insist. I need to do some research on the Net anyway. I can sleep anywhere, and right now, that couch is a pretty damn good option."

"Ah no, you're not sleeping yet. You promised me Thai food and I'm not letting you sleep until you deliver."

"I haven't for—"

A loud knock curtailed Daniel's reply. He moved over and checked through the peephole before he asked who was there.

"Room service."

Beth's face paled as she squeezed her fists tightly, drumming her legs in a nervous gesture. "I didn't order anything," she whispered.

"I did," said Daniel smugly as he opened the door and stood back for the waiter to wheel in the cart. The pungent aromas of coriander and lemongrass filled the room.

Beth just stood there staring with her mouth open and her eyes wide in surprise. "When did you order this?"

The corners of Daniel's eyes creased with amusement. "I can't tell you all my secrets, can I? Where's the fun in that?"

Beth glanced first at Daniel, then at the food. She inhaled the delicious aromas coming from the plates and shrugged. "What the heck. Let's just eat," she said as she limped over, pulled out a chair and sat down.

"Will that be all, sir?" asked the waiter as he shuffled from foot to foot, obviously having somewhere better to be.

"Beth? Would you like anything else?" Daniel asked as he winked at the waiter.

Beth lifted the plate covers and inspected the meal eagerly. "No thanks, this will be fine," she replied. She shook out her napkin and placed it haphazardly across her lap, clearly anxious to get started.

Daniel tipped the waiter while walking him to the door, locking and bolting it behind him. Already seated at the dining cart, Beth tucked in to the meal, oblivious to Daniel's approach.

"So you really like Thai food then?"

Beth swallowed quickly and blushed. "I know I'm greedy, but I promise I'll leave you plenty. It's just that I can't function without food, and it's been a long time since lunch."

"Go ahead. Don't worry about me. I can order more. It's refreshing to find a woman who likes her food. Most women I meet eat like sparrows." Daniel winked at Beth as he sat down. "And a healthy appetite doesn't seem to have done you any harm."

Beth almost choked on her mouthful and grabbed her glass of water quickly to smother the cough. "Thanks," she said, blushing once again and waving her hand back and forth in front of her face. "I think."

Oh great. Not only does he think I'm a stupid woman, now he thinks I'm a glutton. It doesn't matter, does it? Isn't that what she wanted to happen? That he didn't find her attractive and backed off? Of course that's what she wanted...or was it?

"So how did you know my favorite Thai dishes?" asked Beth, trying to steer the conversation onto a safer path.

"Just a lucky guess," he chuckled as he sat down and started eating. "And they're my favorites, too, so I guess we have something in common."

"Really? Something in common?" said Beth, pausing between mouthfuls. "Now that's a surprise."

"Why? Is it that much of a stretch to find some common ground?"

She placed her fork down and looked up. "It's just that our lives are so different. I'm a receptionist, for goodness' sake. How boring is that? And you? Well, you lead this exciting life running around catching bad guys. There's no comparison, really."

Daniel flinched as he sat stiffly back in his chair. "This isn't what I do. Not for a long time anyway. I'm a strategic analyst. I help plan strategies. I'm not a field agent anymore."

"Not a field agent? So why are you here now?"

Pausing briefly, Daniel sighed. "I was in the wrong place at the wrong time. I had no choice."

"Oh." Beth slumped forward, resting her forehead in her hands as she sighed. "I'm so sorry. It's all my fault. If I hadn't been on the train with you—"

"It would have happened anyway," Daniel cut in. "I was already on that train, remember? It's not your fault."

"But if I hadn't gotten you involved... You told me that I asked you to help. If I'd gone for the conductor instead, you would have been left out of it."

"And we wouldn't know that the conference was a target. I *was* on the train and that was enough to make them suspicious of me. There's nothing you could have done that would have made either of us any safer than we are now, so quit beating yourself up."

Daniel leaned across the table and took hold of Beth's hands. A searing heat infused her fingertips, sending tingles through her whole body. Daniel caught her eyes in his gaze and continued, "It's all wasted energy right now. We need to concentrate on finding out who the double agent is and what this means to the Heads of Government Conference, if anything. We only have a few days."

It took all the willpower Beth could muster to talk, her voice shaky as she answered. "You're right, of course. But where do we start? Who knows about me? And how many people know what you're doing?"

Daniel released her hands and a cool breeze from the air conditioning flowed across her skin making her shiver.

"I've thought about that," he said, staring at his hands as he placed them back on the table's edge. "There are three people—my boss, Will Johnson—the helicopter pilot—and you. I can't believe it could be either of them. I've known both of them for years and I'd trust them with my life. It has to be someone else."

"Well, I know it's not me. Maybe someone planted a bug on one of them…or hacked into their email or something."

"You watch too many TV shows. Our security system would detect anything like that. No, it had to be something or someone else." Daniel grunted as he dropped his knife and fork and stood so abruptly Beth jumped in her place. Deep in thought, he crossed the room to the window. The room overlooked Lake Burley Griffin — the city lights reflected off the surface, leaving long, shimmering trails of white across the water. The effect was breathtaking, but Daniel saw nothing at all. His mind was working overtime as he stared into space.

Damn! Where do I start? He shrugged and forced himself out of his reverie, moving toward his knapsack.

"I'd better check in. My boss gets testy if I don't keep him up to speed."

"But what if he's the one who's giving away our position?" asked Beth.

"That's exactly why I need to contact him. So there's no suspicion — not that I do suspect him — but we have to assume everyone is the enemy until we get to the bottom of this."

Daniel removed the small black box from his knapsack and plugged it into his mobile phone. "I'll use several scramblers. No one can trace us from here with them in place." He pressed in a number and moved the phone to his ear. It answered after only two rings.

"Addison?"

"Wyatt! Where the hell have you been? I was expecting your update hours ago."

"Sorry John, that little distraction I mentioned took longer to resolve than I originally thought."

"What's happening there? Is the Hamilton woman still with you?"

"Yes, she's still safe. We plan on lying low until after the Conference. Then we'll come in and finish the investigation."

"Maybe you should come in now."

Daniel paused for just a heartbeat. "No, I don't think that's wise at the moment. You yourself said we should be out of the way so we wouldn't alert the terrorists that we're onto them."

"But they're already onto us. They found you at the safe house. Come in, Daniel. We can keep you safe."

Daniel took in some air and stared out of the window once more. "No, I think we can do much better if we stay out of sight. Remember, apart from the people I report to, most of the department thinks I'm still on sick leave. It'll definitely send up a red flag if I suddenly turn up working on a case."

The silence at the end of the phone was deafening except for a faint static.

"John? You still there?"

"Yes...I was thinking about what you said. There is some merit in what you say. I'll give you some leeway for the moment, but if you have any problems, any problems at all, I want you to come in. Is that understood?"

Daniel slumped in relief. "Perfectly. Thanks, boss. I owe you one."

"Just remember, I always insist on debts being repaid. Check in at the arranged times from now on, will you?"

"Sure thing, boss."

Beth walked slowly toward where Daniel stood. "So?"

"So what?" Daniel smiled.

"What did he say? Was he acting suspicious?"

"No, I don't think so. But we still have to be careful. No one is in the clear until we get to the bottom of this."

Beth carefully sat down in the chair at the desk, rubbing her leg as she descended.

Daniel cursed softly and moved to her side.

"I'm sorry. I forgot about your leg. Can I get you some ibuprofen or an ice pack or something?"

"It's all right, just throbbing a little. I forgot about it, too. It seems to be moving a little more freely now. I guess running away from bad guys is good for it," Beth joked as she stood up and hobbled her way to the bathroom.

Her leg must hurt like hell. But she seemed determined to keep him from helping her at every turn. Damn, she was stubborn. And she was gorgeous, a little annoying sometimes, but gorgeous all the same. All that brilliant red hair, those fiery green eyes and legs that went on forever. *Don't go there.*

Focus, that's what he needed. It took only a few minutes to set up the laptop and plug in the modem. Getting into the department site unnoticed took a few more. Luckily, Daniel had designed the security for the site, so he knew how to get in through a back door. By the time the sound of the shower penetrated, he was skimming personnel files and quickly developing a throbbing headache.

She's in the shower.

The images this revelation provoked ended any hope of Daniel getting anything useful done tonight. *Well, so much for research.* The steam escaping from under the door and the whistling sound as the water sprayed through the faucet conjured up incredibly erotic images. Images of steamy water trickling over a beautiful upturned face. Of hands working soapy lather over a slender body. Of perfect rounded breasts.

Of *his* hands working soapy lather over *her* perfect, rounded breasts, and farther south. *Oh yeah.* How he would've liked to explore that luscious body and lick his way down her body and make her shout with pleasure. *Did the heat get turned up in this room?* Daniel shook his head as his jeans got unbearably tight. *Think with your head, not your pants, buddy!*

Jesus! He'd known this was going to be difficult, but he'd thought he could handle it. *Hah! Fat chance.* He needed to control his urge to give in to his first impulse, which was to join her in that shower and make love to her until they both collapsed. He needed to stay focused until they'd found out who was giving their position away. Beth's life was on the line and he couldn't afford any distractions. Hadn't he already learned a hard lesson with Lisa? A deadly lesson? He'd promised himself that would never happen again. The problem was that he didn't just desire her body—he actually liked Beth...a lot. He shoved a hand through his unruly hair and started pacing. *Get focused, Daniel, and fast.*

He crossed the room to the bar and poured himself a few fingers of Scotch. He stared through the window at the city lights, but all he could see was a vision of Beth in the shower floating in front of him again. *Bloody hell!* This was worse than he'd thought.

* * * *

Beth leaned against the closed bathroom door and grimaced. *Great. Idiot, glutton and invalid. Can I be any more unattractive?* Her leg started aching again but after shedding her clothes, she'd managed to climb over the edge of the bath, even though it had been an exercise in torture.

Shit.

Why didn't a five-star hotel have a separate shower recess, especially a suite? The black marble and the chrome faucets gave the appearance of opulence, but the shower was still over the bath. *Just my luck.*

The warmth of the shower helped a little, but Beth regretted not taking more painkillers when she'd had the chance. What she wouldn't have done for a leg massage like the ones her physical therapist gave her.

Maybe she could ask Daniel? Scratch that. That would be more than she could take. It definitely wouldn't work if she gritted her teeth and thought of something unpleasant this time. It'd defeat the purpose anyway. She was way past diversionary therapy. She thought about what it would feel like if Daniel was rubbing and kneading her stiff muscles, moving up and down her leg. She closed her eyes and saw Daniel join her in the shower. In her dream vision he stood behind her, pulling their bodies together and blowing his hot breath into her ear. Her body tingled with sensation at the very thought of him touching her. She imagined his hands moving around to her groin and softly rubbing the soapy water into her folds, building up a rhythm as she moved her fingers back and forth over her swollen sex. Swaying slightly, she lost her balance and started sliding. She grabbed blindly for the small rail on the far wall. *Oh shit!* She slipped completely over and landed heavily on her back, sprawled along the length of the bath.

The door crashed open and in an instant, Daniel was there. "Are you all right?"

Feeling a hot flush spreading all over her, Beth attempted to pull the shower curtain over her very wet and *very* exposed body.

"I think so. I just slipped," she choked out.

Daniel strode over to the bath and handed her a towel from the rack.

"Give me your hand. I'll get you out."

"No, that's okay, I'll be all right in a minute," said Beth, valiantly attempting to cover herself with the tiny hotel version of a bath towel and trying to look anywhere but at Daniel's face.

God, I'm such a klutz!

"Don't be an idiot. You can't possibly get up without help. Your leg's injured, remember?"

"How could I forget? It's what got me into this mess. I lost my balance and slipped."

Daniel leaned over and, instead of taking Beth's outstretched hand, reached out and scooped her up in one deft move, leaving her breathless and stunned. She barely had time to cover herself again with the wayward towel. She could feel the imprints of his hands as they seared her skin with heat. In an instant she found herself in the bedroom and gently lowered to the bed.

"Thanks, Daniel, I appreciate you rescuing me, but I probably could have managed," she said, as she quickly adjusted the towel to cover herself. *Stupid towel! God, if only he hadn't touched me.*

Daniel frowned as he stood back from the bed and shook his head. "Sure you could have."

"You're right. Thanks for picking me up."

Daniel's eyes glittered with some unspoken emotion. He held out his hand as if to touch her face, but dropped it to his side. He drew in a breath and blew it out slowly. "Look, Beth. I was just trying to help you. Do we need to continue this? I'd better get back to my research."

"I'm sorry. I don't know why I do that. I'm such a grump sometimes. I really do appreciate you helping me."

Daniel's expression softened slightly. "It's okay. I understand."

"I mean, it's my problem, really. Please don't take it the wrong way. I'm like this with everyone." She stopped talking, covering her mouth with her fingers. "Oh God, I'm blabbering now, aren't I?"

"It's okay, really," said Daniel, his face tight. "Do you need anything before I get back to my work?"

"No, I'm fine. I think I'll go to bed now. Goodnight."

Daniel hesitated for a few seconds, his gaze flickering over her exposed body before returning to her face. Was that desire she saw in his eyes? *Don't be stupid. Of course it isn't.* She had an ugly purple scar down the side of her knee. *How much of a turn-on is that?*

"Goodnight then. If you need anything, just call."

"Okay," said Beth, but she was speaking to the air, as Daniel had already left, closing the door behind him.

Daniel couldn't get out of the room fast enough. *That went well,* he told himself. *Yeah, right!* How the hell was he supposed to get focused now? Beth's body was everything he'd dreamed of. Better, even. He imagined himself touching her, tasting her, losing himself in her, no—fucking her brains out! He was going crazy just thinking about her. *Oh shit…this is probably a really bad idea,* he told himself as he turned around and walked purposefully toward the bedroom door. If he could just have one taste…

Beth let out a breath and sighed. How could she have let that happen? Obviously, she had to work harder at ignoring how Daniel affected her. She couldn't afford to let the man mean something. Just because he was the most gorgeous man she'd ever laid eyes on...and kind and smart and funny. He *was* a control freak... Well, he was used to getting his own way, at least, and she was used to going it alone.

She had to keep hold of her independence. It was who she was. No man was going to mess that up. It had taken her long enough to perfect it. No, it would be better not to let it get that far. Better to ignore these feelings before they got out of hand. But that fantasy session in the shower and the heated imprints where his hands had held her made ignoring him an impossible task. Sighing again, she wrapped the towel snugly around her and started to stand.

The door opened again, startling Beth into slipping back onto the bed. In seconds Daniel stood in front of her, his eyes blazing.

"Was there something else?" asked Beth, her mouth suddenly dry.

"Yes, just one more thing..." he said as he pulled her to her feet. "This."

And his mouth captured hers.

Chapter Six

Crash and burn. That was the only way Beth could describe kissing Daniel. From the instant their lips collided, she was overcome with sensual heat. Electric currents flowed from her lips into her chest, gently stroking her heart before coursing down her quivering body. She sighed and opened her mouth to him. He accepted her invitation, his tongue joining hers in a sensuous dance. He tasted of Scotch whisky, all fire. He took control and she let him. *Yes.* This was what she'd been wanting ever since she'd first laid eyes on him across the carriage on the train.

He drew her body close to his, softness to muscle, breast to chest, hip to hip. Her arms moved of their own volition to slide around his neck, and she tangled her fingers in the softness of his tousled hair. She felt his large, thick arousal as he leaned into her body, his heart beating a loud tempo against her chest. *Oh God, he is so big.*

Daniel moved his hand down to her shoulder and slowly stroked a trail down her back, spreading heat in his wake. Her towel dropped noiselessly to the floor and she willed herself closer, molding herself to his shape.

Unable to control her overwhelming emotions, Beth drew away and kissed a trail along his jawline and down his neck. His spiky, unshaven face tickled her skin, increasing her tingling awareness of him. He tasted so good. So salty. So musky. So…Daniel. He moaned at her gentle touch and in return lifted her chin and captured her mouth once more, delving deeper and deeper, claiming her as his own.

He slid his hands up to her breasts, gently kneading and rubbing his thumbs against her peaked nipples and sending jolts of sensation through her.

We shouldn't be doing this. Hadn't she just told herself this? But how could she stop?

No, don't stop!

She'd been kissed before, but never like this. This was more than just sex. She was giving him her heart, and in return he created sensations and feelings she'd never thought possible.

But reality continued to intrude on these feelings, and if anything, Beth was a realist. She didn't even know this man. There was no future in this. *Stop now. Stop before he breaks my heart.*

Beth pulled away and clumsily grabbed for the towel.

Daniel stared at her, his eyes still raw with passion. Seconds ticked by before he spoke.

"I'm not going to apologize," he said before dropping onto the bed, his breathing as ragged as if he'd run a marathon. "If that's what you want, forget it!"

Stunned, Beth moved her hand up to her heart. She turned away, took in a really deep breath and blew it out slowly. "I've never done anything like that before, Daniel. I'm living on adrenaline right now and I don't know what to think. There must be a good reason why we shouldn't have done that, but none comes to mind just yet."

"I can't think of any reason at the moment either, but I'm sure if we try really hard, we'll talk ourselves into something."

Beth turned back and gasped as she found Daniel standing directly in front of her once more.

"Look, I meant it when I said I wasn't sorry. I'm not." He placed his hands on her shoulders and lightly kissed her forehead. "But I am sorry if you've got the wrong impression."

Beth looked up at him and felt a shutter close over her heart. Obviously this meant something different to him. She felt like a fool.

His face tight, Daniel released her. "It was enjoyable, a reaction to the circumstances. But that's all it was, so we should keep it in perspective."

She felt sick. All the air left her lungs. This was what she'd been frightened of. It was obvious he was attracted to her, but it was also obvious that it didn't mean a thing to him. After all this mess was over, so would they be. Over, that was. Praying for courage, Beth dragged in some air and sat back down on the bed, staring at the floor.

"Of course. We let the circumstances take over for a minute. Don't worry. It won't happen again. Let's forget about it," said Beth flatly.

Daniel started walking to the door slowly, but stopped and turned around. "Beth, this probably was a bad idea. You said that yourself. We're going to have to try working together without this messing up our working relationship. Do you think you can do that?"

"Yes." *No...I don't know.*

Although her heart was in a vise, she had no choice. It was either that or risk more pain. She needed to concentrate on getting out of this situation and returning to her normal life.

"I want to call a friend and let him know I'll be staying away for a few more days."

Daniel nodded and handed Beth the mobile phone. "Here, use this so you won't be traced. Hang on a sec while I get the scramblers set up," he said before leaving the room.

Beth sighed as she hurriedly pulled on the robe she'd laid out before her shower. Feeling less exposed but still shaky, she made her way to the sitting room to join Daniel and make her call.

* * * *

Daniel watched Beth closely as she spoke on the phone. Her calm voice as she spoke to her friend belied the stiffness in her body and the clenched fist she tapped on her thigh as she spoke.

He'd wanted just one taste, and he'd gotten it. But he'd never expected a kiss to be so hot. No, not just a kiss, it was more than that—more like spontaneous combustion. He shivered, remembering how her whole body had trembled at his touch. And her skin...so soft, like satin. Who would have thought she would react with such passion? Thank God she'd put on the brakes or they'd probably be on that bed burning the sheets right now.

Damn, but it was good.

How the hell was he going to keep his hands off her now? But he had to. He couldn't let his emotions affect his judgment. He'd been there before and look where that'd gotten him. Someone he'd cared for had died because he'd lost his objectivity. And he'd been left with a desk job dealing with politicians ever since.

That was five years ago, but it still haunted him. He'd been cleared of all wrongdoing in the investigation. They'd said he couldn't have changed the outcome and it wasn't his fault, but he knew differently. He'd been distracted. He'd known he was getting too involved with Lisa, but he hadn't done anything to stop it.

It won't happen again. He wouldn't let it.

Beth ended her phone call and handed Daniel the phone.

"I told him I needed more time away to get my head together and it'd be a few more days."

"Did he buy it?"

"I'm not sure. He seemed to, but he asked a lot of questions. I think I convinced him. The good news is that no one has been around asking about me." Beth leaned against the door frame to the bedroom, her shoulders slumped. "I don't know how long I can keep this up. I hate lying."

"It gets easier."

"I guess you've had a lot of practice."

The fleeting expression of pain and the flatness of her voice showed Daniel just how much she was affected by what had happened between them.

Damn. He hadn't wanted her to get hurt. But it was better to nip whatever feelings they had between them in the bud before she was hurt even more. Or worse still, in more danger because he couldn't get his act together. If only she didn't look so upset.

"Beth…"

Beth straightened her shoulders and walked straight past Daniel. The scent of spring flowers lingered as she turned to him, her face a pale mask.

"Forget it, Daniel. I have, or at least I will have very soon. What's on the agenda for tomorrow then? Do I need to set the alarm?"

"No need. You can sleep in if you want. I need to do a few things tomorrow, so I thought we'd stay put for at least a day."

"Shouldn't we stay out of sight?"

"*You* should stay out of sight. I can look after myself. Remember, I do this for a living."

Beth let out an exasperated sigh. "Of course, how could I forget? Mr. Desk Job to the rescue."

"I didn't always have a desk job, Beth."

Beth lifted her head with a strange expression in her eyes. It seemed as if she was about to voice what was on her mind, but opted at the last moment to say something else. "You mentioned that before," she said, shrugging her shoulders. "One day you'll have to tell me all about it. At the moment, I don't really care. I just need to sleep now. Goodnight, Daniel."

"Goodnight," said Daniel to the bedroom door as Beth shut it softly.

* * * *

The sound of running water brought Daniel awake with a jolt. It was still dark in the room, but a glimmer of light was just visible through the drapes.

A glance at his watch told him it was still early. It seemed that Beth hadn't slept well either. It'd been a rough night. After attempting to go through files for hours, Daniel had found that he wasn't even reading the words. He'd been reliving all of it—her incredible body, her unique scent, the fire and passion, the touch of her lips, the silken feel of her skin. Oh yes, he remembered everything. Everything including the guilt he'd felt when he'd seen the wounded look in her eyes as he told her the kiss didn't mean anything. *What a blatant lie that was.*

It had been a hell of a night. Research had been out of the question. Sleep had been nigh impossible. He'd only managed to doze off at all because of the three Scotches he'd downed in rapid succession after Beth had gone to bed. Waking up now with a heavy head and a dry mouth reminded him of why he hadn't had a drink in a year.

He threw off the blanket and sat up slowly, rubbing his throbbing temples as he reached an upright position. He'd just pulled on his T-shirt when the bedroom door opened.

"Oh…you're up," said Beth as she entered the sitting room, fully dressed.

"Do you have to shout?" Daniel cringed.

Beth stifled a smile as she moved over to the kettle and switched it on. *Good.* He'd had a bad night, too. *Serves him right.* It was all his own doing. Turning back to him, she asked, "Coffee?"

"Sure, whatever…" Daniel said as he continued rubbing his forehead.

Beth opened the foil packets of coffee and put them in the two cups that she found in the cupboard.

"Rough night?"

"I've had better," barked Daniel. He stood up now and stretched his arms over his head. Beth drew in a breath as she took in his magnificent torso. His T-shirt lifted and revealed a washboard stomach with a light sprinkling of brown hair thickening as it reached his shorts. She found herself staring until the electric kettle boiled, which thankfully gave her a legitimate reason to turn away.

Stop it, Beth.

Her hands shook as she poured the boiling water, almost spilling the hot liquid onto the countertop. So much for the promises she'd made herself during her sleep-deprived night. *Get that thought out of your mind right now,* she berated herself. *He's made himself perfectly clear. The kiss was just a little fun. Nothing more.* She had to stop turning to mush every time she was near him.

Straightening, she picked up his cup and offered it to him. "You have it black, right?"

"Thanks."

She carefully avoided touching his hand as she handed over his coffee, noticing that he seemed to be doing the same thing. *Good, he's avoiding me, too. I can live with that. But only if it's the physical contact.* She thought about the predicament they were in. There was no way he was going to shut her out of that. She wasn't used to sitting back while someone else did the work.

"So tell me," she asked. "Who's this person you have to see today?"

"A friend."

Beth rolled her eyes. He was trying to cut her out of the loop. Just like she'd thought he would. "A friend? That tells me a lot."

"The less you know, the safer you'll be."

"Yeah, right! I have just as much at stake as you do. Probably more. It's me they want, not you. So don't think for one minute that I don't want to be involved here. I've spent the last five years cleaning up my own messes and I'm not going to stop now just because Mr. Desk Job wants to cut me out of the loop." Okay, so she was laying it on a bit thick. She wasn't usually such a bitch, but she was still raw from last night.

He narrowed his eyes. She could almost see sparks coming out of them. He was pissed. *Well, too bad, so am I. Get over it, bud.*

"And I've spent the last five years making sure that people like you keep safe, so you can just stay put and let me do my job!"

What is he saying? People like me? Beth's mind went into overdrive. There was something he wasn't telling her. Some reason why he wouldn't let her in. An idea began forming in her head, but she had to think very carefully about what she said next.

"Okay, maybe I can stay here, but I can still help you. I'm pretty good with computers. You could get me into the files at your office. Maybe I could find something. And what about the files of that man who was killed? They might tell us something about who these people are."

Daniel shook his head and smiled. "You don't give up, do you? Okay, I'll have a shower and we'll discuss this. Meanwhile, how about ordering some breakfast? I know you think better on a full stomach."

"Ouch! You really know how to make a girl feel special," she said, as she picked up the room service menu. "Any requests?"

"No, I'll leave that to you," he said as he grabbed his backpack and headed for the bathroom.

* * * *

Eating breakfast gave Daniel time to calm down, considering their discussion moments before. Daniel watched Beth as she concentrated on her plate, enjoying with obvious relish the poached eggs and bacon she'd ordered for them both. He narrowed his eyes as she took a sip of her coffee before she turned toward him and smiled. *What is she up to? She couldn't be planning on leaving the hotel, could she? She'd better not be.*

"You understand why you can't come with me, don't you?" asked Daniel, not liking the smug expression he saw on her face.

"Yes, I know. I might be recognized," she answered. "But how are you going to get by without being seen? This is your home town, after all."

"It's easier for me to blend into the background. All it takes is a baseball cap, a pair of sunglasses and a good set of eyes."

"If you say so."

"Beth, I've done this sort of thing before, and with the exception of three people, people think I'm on leave and out of town," he said. "No one is expecting to see me, and people only take notice of what they're expecting."

"It's that simple?"

"Trust me. It is," he said.

"Well, you'd better show me how to get into the files before you go," said Beth, wiping her mouth with her napkin as she stood.

Daniel watched her hand slide over those lips, and fought a shiver as he remembered his own mouth had touched those same lips the previous night. He turned away quickly, but not fast enough. Beth blushed as she noticed the direction his eyes had taken.

Get a hold of yourself, Daniel. Not now, stick to the business at hand. Bracing himself, he stood and walked over to the laptop, turning it on. Beth joined him and listened as he explained how to scroll through the public service department files.

"How do I get inside Peter Wilson's diary? I might be able to find out who he was meeting with on a regular basis up until the train crash."

"I'll have to go to the system manager's file first, since his files have been retired for the duration of the investigation." After typing in a series of numbers and letters, Daniel brought up a number of icons, clicked on one and immediately a version of Outlook filled the screen. "Hang on a sec... There you go."

"That's amazing. So we can add hacking to your repertoire," she said.

Daniel grinned at her. "Just another one of my many talents."

"You're getting quite a collection," said Beth. She stared at him as his mouth began to curl into a smile. *She has such expressive green eyes.* Turning away, he stood and walked over to the wardrobe. He carried one of the backpacks over to the table, then opened it to pull out a couple of pairs of sunglasses and several baseball caps. He picked one of each, zipped the bag and threw it back in the cupboard.

"Lock the door when I leave."

"I will." She smiled up at him as she seated herself in front of the laptop.

He gave her a penetrating glare, hoping he succeeded in letting her know he meant business. "And don't answer the door for anyone, not even people you know, unless it's me."

"I won't."

"And don't answer the hotel phone. If I have to contact you, I'll call this one," he said as he handed her a small silver mobile device. "And if you need me at all, for anything, just press one and it'll get me."

"Okay, I get it," she said as she started tapping on the keyboard. "No contact with anyone except you. Now you can go. I'll be fine."

"All right then. I'll bring some food back with me. I think it will be better if we limit our exposure to the hotel staff. Raid the minibar if you get hungry."

"Don't worry. I will," she said. "Now go, so you can bring me lunch at a reasonable hour."

He nodded and turned for the door. Briefly the thought crossed his mind that she was giving in too easily. He hoped not. She'd better stay put. There wasn't time to go traipsing after her if she got into more trouble. And she had to stay safe at all costs. Maybe he should've handcuffed her to the bed. Grinning at the thought, he imagined her eyes flashing with passion and fire. *No way...* That would be too tempting by half. He straightened up and pulled the cap over his head to hide his slightly long brown hair.

"I'll be back as soon as I can."

* * * *

After Daniel had left, Beth collected the breakfast trays and deposited them outside the door. Leaving the 'do not disturb' light on, she locked the door and flipped the chain into place. Time to get to work.

She knew Daniel had been suspicious of her. He'd thought she was up to something. She wasn't, but it amused her that he thought she was. *As if.* She wasn't that stupid. What could she do anyway? She wasn't familiar with Canberra, and she knew no one in the city. Except...maybe she did have one contact. Her parents had had a friend who lived in Canberra, but she'd lost contact with him over the years. She hadn't seen him since the funeral, and she'd been so numb at the time that she couldn't even remember what they'd talked about. She remembered that he'd had a falling out with her father not long before her parents' death, and that her father didn't talk about him after that. Maybe he could help them. He used to work with her father in the Australian Federal Police. He might know what to do. She walked over to the desk, withdrew her address book from her purse and started flipping through the pages.

* * * *

The phone rang in an office high above the city. The silver-haired man hesitated before reaching for the cradle, his fingers tense as he raised it to his ear. He knew exactly who it was on the end of the line. He needed more time. Time he didn't have.

"Is it done?" barked the voice at the end of the line.

"Not yet."

An intake of breath sounded. The voice paused before continuing. "I'm getting impatient. It must be done soon."

"I know. We're getting closer."

"You had better be. You know what will happen if you fail."

The silver-haired man sucked in a breath. He knew exactly what would happen if he failed. He knew what was at stake. He had to prevent that at all costs. "I'm aware of the consequences. It will be done in time."

"Good, see that it is."

* * * *

Daniel crossed the road and entered the hotel through the side door. He'd had a frustrating morning and needed to get to his laptop before he could get any further information. Will hadn't been able to add anything to what he already had. Someone knew their every move. There were no tracking devices on them. He'd checked everything they'd brought with them.

And the Conference was only a few days away. They thought they had it covered. The security had been upgraded to protect the British Prime Minister.

Unless it wasn't the Prime Minister who was the target. If not him, then who? His best bet was those files Beth was checking out. He hoped she'd been able to come up with something. If he could find the leak, he may be able to figure out what this was all about, but they'd better hurry. Time was running out.

As he'd prearranged with Beth, he rang the doorbell when he reached the suite. Nothing. The hairs on his neck pricked up and his gut clenched. A maid peeked out of the room opposite and stared suspiciously at him. Ignoring her, he switched to knocking, then pounded on the white painted wood. Still nothing. He grabbed the handle and tried it. It was locked. He slipped his key card into the slot and shoved the door open. He raced into the suite, where his eyes zeroed in on the desk. The laptop was gone. Listening for any sounds, he carefully walked to the bedroom and opened the door. The bed was neatly made with clean towels sitting on the edge. He stepped through to the bathroom and swore.

She was gone.

Chapter Seven

Beth entered the coffee shop and asked for directions to the ladies room. She smiled, thanked the waitress and ordered a cappuccino before moving past the counter out the back entrance and into the back lane.

Her heart pounded as she looked both ways. Suppressing a twinge of guilt for ordering something she'd had no intention of paying for, she adjusted the cap she wore over the long dark wig she'd pilfered from Daniel's backpack of tricks. No way could anyone have recognized her. She'd never be caught dead in a baseball cap. Anyone who knew her would know that. But of course, whoever was trying to kill her didn't know her as well as her friends did.

She walked up the lane, slowly at first, then gathering momentum as she neared another small lane that veered to the right. Ducking into a doorway, she peered back. She couldn't see anyone, but she could feel someone there. Right now she was wishing she'd stayed put in the hotel. It had seemed like a good idea at the time. She was going stir crazy waiting for Daniel to come back from his meeting, so she thought a short walk wouldn't do any harm. After downloading the files she needed when she'd logged on at the Internet café, all she'd wanted to do was sit in the park and do her research in the sunshine. She'd thought the hat and the wig disguised her pretty well. Obviously not well enough, because she'd only been sitting in the park for about fifteen minutes before she'd felt, rather than seen, someone staring at her. She'd gotten up and moved around the park among the crowd.

The feeling had followed her.

That was how she'd found herself here in this laneway. She couldn't take any chances. Daniel wasn't going to be happy when he found out. In fact, she imagined that he was furious right about now. Now if she could only figure out how to get herself back to the hotel, which at the moment was clearly a challenge.

A low humming sound interrupted her thoughts. Confused, she turned her head to see where the sound was coming from. It seemed to come from her bag. She patted the bag down to find the source of the buzzing. *Of course, the phone!* Beth retrieved the device Daniel had given her and braced for what was coming.

"Daniel, I can explain."

"Where the hell are you?"

"In a doorway."

"Doorway? Where?"

"In an alley behind a coffee shop."

Beth moved the phone away from her ear as a few choice expletives came through the line.

She heard footsteps coming toward her. "Look, Daniel," she whispered. "You can shout at me later, okay? I think I'm being followed. I have to go. I'll head back to the hotel when I shake him, otherwise I'll call you."

She pushed the end button, threw the phone in her bag and knocked lightly on the door she stood in front of. As a short Chinese woman opened the door, Beth placed a finger to her lips and sidled past her to the front of the shop. It was an Asian grocer. Thankfully there were a number of customers bartering noisily in their own languages. Beth slipped around them quickly and out onto the street.

There was a taxi rank across the street and a cab pulled up to the curb as she arrived, letting out a passenger.

Thank you, God!

Beth raced over and jumped in, slamming the door behind her. She turned as the taxi sped off in the direction of the hotel and saw a man run out of the shop, looking both ways down the street. *That was too close.*

She retrieved the phone and dialed Daniel.

"Are you all right?"

"I'm fine. I'll be there in a few minutes."

"Good," he said curtly before he hung up on her.

Beth got out of the cab around the corner from the hotel. She slowly walked across the road at the pedestrian lights, trying to check out each person she passed without causing suspicion. Any one of them could be following her. How had someone found her? How had she been recognized? The disguise was good. She knew it was. She'd been certain even her parents, if they were alive, would have had a hard time knowing it was her. If not her looks, then what was it that gave her away? She felt the laptop bump her thigh through the bag she had slung over her shoulder. The laptop? No, it couldn't be. They'd had it with them the whole time. She'd have to ask Daniel if that were possible.

Think. If not the laptop itself, maybe the site she was searching. The appointment diary. It had to be. They must have picked up the signal while she was plugged in at the Internet café. That *had* to be how they'd found her.

She needed to get to Daniel and fast.

As inconspicuously as she could, she raced through the lobby and took the first elevator up to their suite. Trepidation filled her as she reached the room. She knew Daniel was angry with her and she really couldn't blame him. Taking a deep breath, she slipped the card in the slot and placed her hand on the doorknob.

The door jerked open and away from her hand. Daniel dragged her into the room and closed the door firmly.

"What the fuck did you think you were doing?" barked Daniel.

Yep, he's angry all right. May as well tell him the good news now.

"We have to get out of here right away. I'll explain as we go," said Beth as she headed for the bedroom with every intention of packing.

Daniel grabbed her arm again and held her in place. "I've already packed. You can explain in the car. We need to hit the road."

Too stunned to do anything else, Beth nodded and took the bag Daniel handed to her as they headed out of the door. The lift doors opened as they reached the hallway. Signaling her to be silent, Daniel grabbed Beth's hand and pulled her the other way down the corridor and through the fire escape door. Surprising Beth, Daniel led them up the stairs instead of down.

"Where are we going?"

"Up to the walkway to the other tower. We can get to the garage without going through the lobby from there."

Of course, thought Beth. *First rule of secret agents — know your escape routes.* She followed him as best she could, trying not to slow their progress, but her leg had started to ache again. Her limp was getting more marked as they drew closer to the elevators in the adjacent tower. Daniel watched as she rubbed her thigh while they waited for the car to arrive, although he seemed more irritated than concerned. *Boy, he's still mad.*

"Your leg hurting you?"

"It'll be all right. I can manage. We are going for another car trip, right? I can rest it while you drive."

"It'll be a long drive. We can't afford to stop for some time."

"Where are we going? No, scratch that. Surprise me."

Daniel arched his eyebrow and his eyes crinkled at the edges. For a second there Beth thought he was smiling, but it passed as quickly as it started and his face became a mask of determination. Not a smile in sight.

* * * *

Daniel drove carefully around the outskirts of the city. The lunchtime traffic wasn't heavy, but busy enough that he needed to be alert.

How had they been made? Damn stubborn woman! Why hadn't she just stayed put? He'd trusted her, even when he'd known she was giving in too easily. It wouldn't happen again. From now on they'd be joined at the hip. He had to keep her safe, and that was damn near impossible if she went charging off on her own.

But first he had to figure out how they'd been located. He had to admit Beth's disguise had been pretty good. If he hadn't known it was her coming through the door, he wouldn't have recognized her. He needed some answers. She was sitting slumped in the passenger seat and he felt a twinge of guilt. If they'd taken her into protective custody from the start, this wouldn't have happened.

Beth's unruly curls were translucent as the afternoon sun shone through the windscreen, showing sparkling golden highlights. Her green eyes were dull and tired and he noticed the dark circles that were more apparent now, due to the light. She might be a bit reckless, but she was certainly not a shrinking violet. It was an impossible situation, but she had been handling it like a pro—if he discounted her idiocy this morning. She shifted in her seat and took in a deep breath. Her breasts rose and the T-shirt she was wearing stretched tightly, outlining her nipples.

Heat and awareness flooded through Daniel as he remembered the previous night. Those breasts were damn near perfect. He shook his head in a vain attempt to shift the erotic images of his mouth claiming a taut nipple and grazing it with his teeth. He turned his head quickly back to the road, but not quite quickly enough. He saw Beth flush as he heard a catch in her breath. Her eyes widened as she stared at the not-so-subtle bulge in his jeans before jerking her head in the opposite direction.

Good one, Daniel. This is not the time for fantasizing. Get over it. They needed a plan.

* * * *

"So, now would be a good time to fill me in on why you thought it was a good idea to disregard my orders," said Daniel as they sat at the picnic table, eating the burgers they'd bought for lunch.

Beth stopped mid-bite and swallowed. Her face was flushed. She really was beautiful, he thought. Annoying, exasperating, but still beautiful. He had to stop thinking like that—he knew it was dangerous. After the distress he'd seen in her eyes last night, he knew he didn't want to hurt her again.

She turned back, this time making eye contact with him. He didn't see the repentant face he was expecting, but a fierce determination.

"Well, it was lucky I did, because if I'd stayed in the hotel, I would have been a sitting duck," she said.

"What do you mean?"

"He traced me somehow. I think it must have been when I was logged in to the email account. If I'd been in the hotel, I wouldn't have been able to give him the slip."

"Go on..." said Daniel.

"Look, I took precautions. I had myself so well disguised that even my own family wouldn't have recognized me, but *he* did."

"How do you know it was one of the bad guys? It could have just been someone who fancied you."

"I don't think so. An admirer doesn't chase you through a back lane and follow you through a shop out onto the street. I think I can tell the difference."

"Maybe you're right."

"Of course I'm right. What about the person in the hall at the hotel? How did they find us if it wasn't a tracking device?"

Daniel paused to think. He took another bite of his burger and visualized the equipment they had with them. Maybe he missed something, but he wasn't convinced. "It's possible. But I don't think it's from the website. I was working on that most of the night and they didn't find us then. It has to be something else. What did you take with you?"

"The laptop, your phone, the wig and cap. The shoulder bag, my purse…"

All those items were secure, thought Daniel. It had to be something else. He reached for his cola and took a sip before placing it back on the table. "How about you start from the beginning…from when you decided to leave the hotel? Tell me everything that happened — where you went, who you saw. Don't leave anything out."

Beth blinked and stared down at the empty wrapper in front of her. She wiped her fingers and mouth with the napkin, and leaned forward onto the table with her elbows.

"I started to get claustrophobic in that room and I knew I had to get out before I suffocated. I just wanted a change of scenery, Daniel. I didn't mean to stay out long."

Daniel frowned at her but remained silent. Gulping, she continued.

"So I took a wig and hat from your backpack, packed up the laptop and went out."

"Where did you go?"

"I went to that Internet café in the hotel lobby, where I found a private cubicle and plugged in the laptop. Then I logged into the diary again."

Daniel narrowed his eyes. How the hell did she do that? He'd had to hack in. It wasn't an easy task, he knew from first-hand experience. He opened his mouth to speak but she raised her hand for him to let her continue.

"I've been studying computer programming with Open Universities and it seems I have a talent for it."

"I'll say. That site has top-level security attached to it."

Beth blushed again and shifted in her seat. "I remembered what you'd done this morning and tried to reproduce it. It worked. Anyway, I didn't stay logged on for long."

"How long?'

"About fifteen or twenty minutes. I decided I needed fresh air, so I copied the file, packed up and went outside. That's when I found the park."

"Park? That's quite a way from the hotel."

"I needed the exercise. I have to compensate for my appetite somehow." She smiled slightly but Daniel ignored it and continued firing questions.

"Okay, so you went to the park. What happened next?"

"I was sitting on the grass working from the laptop for about fifteen minutes when I started to feel uneasy. I was sure someone was watching me, but I couldn't see anyone."

"I know that feeling. I've learned to trust my instincts."

"Yes, well, I didn't want to take any chances so I headed out the other side of the park. I couldn't shake the feeling I was being followed so I ducked into a coffee shop and slipped out the back door."

Daniel stared at her now. She was smart, but she shouldn't have been there in the first place. Shrugging his shoulders, he resumed his interrogation.

"Did anyone follow you out of the coffee shop?"

Beth's breathing became shorter. Her eyes flashed and for an instant Daniel thought he saw fear, but they cleared quickly as she exhaled deeply.

"I hid in a dark doorway. By this stage my leg was really killing me and I couldn't run. That's when I saw a man searching the alleyway near the coffee shop."

Holy Shit! She could have been killed. He continued to be amazed at her cool head. Gripping his fists under the table, he waited for her to continue.

"So I knocked on the door and raced through the shop into the street. I jumped in a cab and headed back to the hotel. You know the rest."

Daniel swore under his breath and unclenched his fists, splaying his fingers over his thighs. He took a deep breath and blew it out slowly. "Did you see him after that?"

"I saw someone run out of the same shop and look up and down the street. It could have been him, but by that time I was already driving off in the taxi."

Shit. He had to figure out how they'd been found...and fast. Someone could be already on their tail.

"I think it's the laptop," said Beth.

Daniel turned his head, quickly searching her eyes, which were wide and maybe just a little bit frightened.

"You think it has a detection device?"

"I don't know. We've had it all along and they didn't find us at the hotel. Maybe it's the diary website. It could trigger an alarm that enables the server to track the users. They can do that through the ISP."

Daniel stared out over the paddock next to the picnic table. *Maybe she's right. It's certainly possible. But why now and not last night?*

"I accessed that site last night. We weren't tracked then."

Beth shifted forward and brushed an errant red curl behind her ear. "Maybe it took that long to persuade the ISP to cooperate. Don't they need a court order or something?"

Yes, they do. And it would take someone high up in the Federal Police to get one through that quickly. *Damn.* He had to call Addison. It was time he had a talk with him. He needed to find out if there was any new information. Time was running out.

Daniel crushed the empty food containers and stood. "I've got a call to make. Hang about; I won't be long." He threw the rubbish into the bin and continued walking past the table into the bush track behind the picnic area. He pulled out his phone and plugged in the scrambler before punching in a few numbers.

"Addison."

"It's me."

"Wyatt, you're late again. But I trust you have a good excuse."

Daniel hesitated before continuing. "Someone made us."

"What? Is the girl okay?"

"Yes, but only because she's smart." Not smart enough to follow orders though, he added silently. "It could have been a lot worse."

"So, are you clear now?"

He turned back to make sure Beth was still in sight. She was, thankfully. "Yeah, for the moment. I need you to find out something for me."

"Shoot."

Turning away again, he shifted his weight to one leg and leaned against a ghost gum, partially obscuring himself from Beth's view to ensure she couldn't hear the conversation. "Someone got clearance to trace a website to an ISP. I need to know who."

"Is that how they found you?"

"It seems likely, but I'm not sure. I need you to check it out anyway. At the moment, it's our only lead."

"Consider it done. In the meantime, I think you should come in. It's not safe out there for you anymore."

Daniel took the phone from his ear and turned his head back to where Beth sat. He raised it to his ear again and spoke quietly into the phone. "I don't think that's a good idea right now. We've managed to lose them for the time being and whoever this is might be watching our safe houses. Considering they already found us at one."

Addison paused. "All right, I'll agree to that for now. But if you need me, you know where to find me. And, Daniel…"

"Yes?"

"Be careful."

"You know me, boss. I'm always careful."

Daniel jammed the phone back into his pocket and slowly walked back to the picnic table. Beth had already cleared the remaining rubbish and was waiting for him. He unlocked the car and they both got in.

"Where are we going?"

"Sydney."

"Great, I can check up on Dr. Bennett."

Daniel turned to her sharply. "No, you can't talk to anyone you know. They could be watching him."

Beth started to say something, but stopped. She sighed. "I guess you're right. But what if Doc calls the police?"

"You spoke to him yesterday, remember? Everything should be all right for the time being."

Beth nodded. Daniel glanced at her before he started the engine. She was so vulnerable sitting there, leaning her head against the window, her hand cupping her cheek.

"It will be all right, Beth. I promise."

"I hope you're right."

So did he.

* * * *

He was angry. He shouldn't have failed. That girl was smart. Smarter than they'd realized, and they should have known better. It wouldn't happen again. The idiot who'd lost her wouldn't dare. He would pay dearly for another mistake.

The silver-haired man slammed his fist hard on the desk in front of him.

Damn.

Now he didn't have a choice. Everything he'd built over the years would be destroyed unless he did something. He would have to call in the last favor.

Chapter Eight

The quiet, narrow streets of Balmain were a contrast to the traffic they'd driven through for the last hour and a half since arriving in Sydney. The quaint terraces were so small compared to the large family homes of Turramurra where Beth had lived all her life. Daniel parked the car on the wrong side of the street in front of a high sandstone wall.

"Why are you parking that way?"

"This is how everyone parks around here. They call it a 'Balmain' park," he said, as if she should know what that meant, which she didn't. But it didn't really matter. She was curious to see who it was they were there to see.

She followed him through the gate and up to the imposing wooden door. After ringing the doorbell, Daniel turned to her and took her hand.

"It'll be all right, just follow my lead and let me do the talking."

Hearing footsteps approaching, Beth just nodded and pulled her hand back hastily. Someone peered through the peephole at them.

The door opened swiftly and a tall blond man stood in the hallway. His expression was one of extreme shock.

"Danny — Holy shit!"

Daniel chuckled, then pulled Beth's hand and dragged her into the house, pushing past his friend.

"Kevin, it's good to see you too."

"I heard you were out of action."

"Yes, well, you should know you shouldn't always believe what you hear."

"Well, hell, this is fantastic news, but I suspect a long story. Grab a pew. I think I need a drink."

Beth gazed at Daniel and back to his friend as she sat in a large overstuffed chair opposite the couch where Daniel sat. Other than his name, she didn't have a clue who he was. It was obvious they were good friends and Daniel trusted him. He was staring at her now, smiling. His brown eyes held a sparkle and she thought maybe she could trust him, too.

"Daniel? Are you going to introduce me to this gorgeous woman, or do I have to jump in myself?"

Beth saw Daniel stiffen slightly and frown, just for a fleeting moment. He recovered quickly however and his usual devastating smile returned.

"Of course… Kevin, this is Beth Hamilton. Beth, Kevin Donnelly."

Kevin held out his hand and took hers in a firm grip. "Pleased to meet you, Beth."

She retrieved her hand, and smiled. "It's a pleasure to meet a friend of Daniel's."

Kevin laughed. "I suppose you could call us friends, although we've tried to kill each other many times in the past."

"What?"

Daniel glared at Kevin. "He means on the rugby field. I played for Riverview and he played for Joey's."

"Ah…" said Beth, understanding at last. Riverview and St Joseph's, the traditional enemies of the elite private school rugby union competition.

Kevin laughed again, the corners of his eyes crinkling wickedly. "Yes, so you see, Beth, Danny boy and I go way back."

Danny boy? Who would have thought? Beth looked at Daniel again just in time to see him scowl at Kevin. He didn't like that nickname. *Interesting.* Beth filed away that titbit for a rainy day. She caught Kevin staring at her expectantly.

"Beth?"

She blinked. "Sorry. What did you say?"

"I'm crushed, Beth. I don't usually have that effect on women."

"Quit the flirting, Kev. Beth, he asked you what you'd like to drink."

Beth gulped and shifted in her seat. Obviously there was some serious rivalry going on between these old friends. "Sorry, Kevin, I'm just a little tired. A coffee would be great, thanks."

"Okey-dokey…and, Daniel? The usual?"

Daniel nodded as Kevin headed down the hall, presumably to the kitchen. He fell back into the couch and exhaled deeply. Beth could see the tension in the stiffness of his jaw and his hands, which he was clenching and unclenching as if to hold off stiffness. No doubt he was tired as well. The drive from Canberra had taken just over four hours and he hadn't let her take the wheel once. She'd at least dozed a little, but he'd been driving practically nonstop, the whole time alert to see if they'd been followed.

"You've known each other a long time."

"It seems a lifetime. He can help us, Beth, but you have to let me handle what we say. I don't want to draw him in too deep."

"This sounds serious. Don't want to draw me in too deep with what?" said Kevin, as he re-entered the room with a tray of drinks.

"You don't want to know all the details, Kev," said Daniel as he leaned forward. "Suffice it to say I'll fill you in on a need-to-know basis. You should be used to that, considering the crowd you work for."

"Danny, we're friends. You know I'll help all I can," said Kevin, handing Daniel a glass of Scotch.

The sound of a whistling kettle broke the silent tension that had suddenly filled the room. Beth jumped to her feet. She needed some fresh air…and fast.

"I'll get the coffee, Kevin. I'll find my way. You two need to talk."

Daniel gave Beth a tight smile and mouthed a thank you as she exited. Even though she wanted out of there, she still would have loved to hear what Daniel and Kevin were saying.

The hall offered her two choices—the room on the right or the room at the end of the corridor. Beth opted for the end of the corridor, thinking that the kitchen would logically be at the rear of the house.

What greeted her, however, was the furthest thing from a kitchen she'd ever seen. Two of the walls were covered in books, some fallen sideways in their shelves, the others stacked up horizontally, as if there was not enough room for them all. The third wall was awash with technology. A large, flat computer screen sat on a desk that was scattered with files and papers. A fax machine, printer and scanner sat on a smaller table to the side of the desk. A window from floor to ceiling, offering a view of a small patio garden. But that was not what caught Beth's attention. It was the cover of one of the files on the desk. There, in plain writing for all to see, was the logo for ASIO — the Australian Securities Intelligence Organization. Kevin Donnelly, Daniel's friend, was a spy.

Beth quietly closed the door as she left and moved to the other room, which thankfully *was* the kitchen. Thinking about it, it probably wasn't a bad thing to discover. Having someone with Kevin's connections could be an advantage, as long as it didn't get him in trouble with his superiors. That must be what Daniel meant by getting in too deep. She didn't like the idea of anyone else embroiled in her troubles. She wanted to think of a way to get out of it herself, but she wasn't so stupid as to think she didn't need help from people who were used to dealing with this sort of thing.

She carried her steaming cup into the room to join the men. They both stopped talking as she entered. She felt as if she was intruding.

Well, bad luck. It was her life they were discussing and it was her right to be involved in whatever they were planning.

"Danny tells me you've had a bit of an adventure over the last few months," said Kevin, as she sat back in her chair.

She took a sip of her coffee and placed it on the table in front of her before she answered.

"One that I'd rather not have had, I can assure you."

"I can understand that. I'm sorry. I didn't mean to be flippant."

"I didn't think you were."

"Beth, Kevin is going to help keep you safe while we sort this all out," interrupted Daniel.

"What? You're going to hide me away while you get to play your spy games? This is my life we're talking about here. Don't I get a say in how it plays out?"

She glared at Daniel then shifted her gaze to Kevin. Okay, so that was probably too much, but it was too late now. She'd already said it.

He placed his hands in the air in mock defeat. "Hey, don't look at me. It was all Danny boy's idea."

"Thanks so much for your support, Kevin," said Daniel through gritted teeth. "Beth, you're in over your head with this. You should to leave it to us. We have the connections and the resources. You don't."

Ouch. What he said was true, thought Beth as she slumped back into the chair. But it still didn't mean that she couldn't have a say in what happened to her. She wasn't stupid and she had damn good computer skills. And she'd done a pretty good job at protecting herself this morning in Canberra.

"I agree I don't have the resources you have, but I still think I can help. I didn't do so bad this morning, did I? And I don't like decisions being made about me without being consulted."

"What happened this morning?" asked Kevin.

Realizing she'd probably said too much, Beth fell silent.

Kevin glared at Daniel then Beth. "Well, is someone going to tell me what happened? I'm really curious now."

"I—"

"Let me handle this, Beth," cut in Daniel. "She was followed and managed to get away. That's why we hightailed it out of town and came here."

"How the hell did they find you?"

"We need to find out. Then we'll be able to work out the whos and whys of it. That's why I need access to a secure computer and for you to make some discreet inquiries."

"I'll do everything I can, mate. Just ask."

"That's what I'd hoped you say. First thing I need is to get Beth out of sight. I want her safe."

Beth was stunned. He was shutting her out again and she couldn't let that happen. Not if she could help it.

"What about you, Daniel? They're after you, too. Who's going to keep you safe?" said Beth, her voice rising.

She could almost see fiery sparks coming from Daniel's eyes as he glared at her and began to speak. But before the first word left his lips, Kevin burst into laughter.

"I fail to find any humor in this, Kevin," said Daniel

"Sorry, mate, it's just that now I see why you want to get Beth under wraps."

"What the heck is that supposed to mean?" demanded Beth.

Daniel stood up, grabbing the car keys from the table. "I don't have time for this right now, Beth. Kevin, I need to get rid of the car. I'll bring in our gear and go."

"Wait a minute, Daniel. We haven't finished talking yet," said Beth, following him toward the door.

"I have. Remember, Kevin and I are the pros here. We know what we're doing. Stay put. I'll be back in a couple of hours, maybe sooner."

"No problem, Danny. Beth and I'll get acquainted while you're gone. It's been a while since I had such a beautiful woman in my pad."

Daniel flinched and inhaled sharply.

"I find that hard to believe, Kevin. I'm sure you'll keep her company for me. You do remember how to do that, don't you?"

"Of course," said Kevin, a glint of humor in his eyes. "Beth and I will be joined at the hip until you get back."

* * * *

Daniel slammed the car door shut just as he turned the key in the ignition and drove away. He needed speed. He couldn't think while Beth was around. She was so exasperating, so reckless. *So damn beautiful.* Fuck, she didn't need him distracted. She could wind up dead.

Like Lisa.

He drummed his fingers on the steering wheel while he waited at the traffic lights. But Beth wasn't Lisa. This was different. He'd never felt this way about Lisa. They'd been friends. They'd cared about each other, but this was more than that. Every time he thought about her he felt hot. And after that kiss…*whoa!*

The blast of a horn jolted Daniel back to reality. *Damn!* This was what he'd been trying to avoid. Shaking himself, he put the car in gear and drove on a little too forcefully. The property where he was meeting Will was about forty minutes out of town. After he exchanged cars again, he was hoping he could get some answers. Maybe Will had some ideas as to who may be leaking their position to the bad guys, whoever they were. After the train crash it had been pretty much accepted that they knew who the target was—the British Prime Minister. But now he wasn't so sure. And, until they'd confirmed who they were dealing with, Beth was in extreme danger.

* * * *

The sun was low and darkness was not far away when Daniel took a right turn off the main road from Dural and passed two large properties. *Man, there is some big money living around here.* At the end of the road he continued on a dirt track until he came to a driveway, partially hidden by the thick undergrowth and a couple of gum tree saplings, which he swerved to avoid.

The gate to the property was open as he drove through, but he stopped to close it before continuing on. The house — if he could call it a house — was small like a cabin, and old. The paint job on the worn weatherboards showed the original owners were well acquainted with the sixties. Each board was a different color, ranging from faded purple to green and orange, and peeling much like the fruit. The front door had a large flower painted on the middle panel. The porch posts were covered with an overgrown creeper, twisting and falling over the edges of the veranda.

The scent of jasmine was almost overpowering as Daniel cautiously got out of the car. Where the hell was Will? He should have heard him pull up, so why didn't he come out to meet him?

The hairs on the back of his neck stood to attention. Something wasn't right here. He surveyed the land around the house. Nothing was obvious at this stage as Daniel concentrated on the sounds around him. All he could hear was the chirping of the native birds that made their home in the bush, and the distant sound of traffic from the highway.

He cursed himself for not recovering his Glock from the gear he'd left with Kevin. Not being a field agent anymore meant that he didn't have clearance to carry a weapon, except in extreme emergencies, and he sure as hell hadn't expected trouble here with Will. What a stupid decision that had been. Someone seemed to be following his every move. He should have known better.

He scanned the ground for anything that could double as a weapon. He spotted a block of wood over near the step to the veranda. The termites had gotten to it, but he picked it up anyway. He hit the wood against his palm to test, and it didn't disintegrate. It'd do until he found something better.

There was a small wooden building just visible to the right of the house. It could be a storage shed or even a garage. He listened carefully as he walked toward the double doors. They were locked with a rusting chain and padlock. He pulled on it firmly. Locked tight. He peered through a crack between the two doors. A late model Subaru Outback was parked inside, but it took up so much room he couldn't see anything else.

Turning to his left, he spied the rear entrance to the house. The ancient screen door was open and the door behind ajar. He approached it slowly, checking from side to side as he went, listening hard for any sound of unwanted company.

The house was silent. Entering the kitchen, he took in the signs of occupation. There was an open loaf of bread and a jar of peanut butter on the counter. A coffee cup sat next to an electric kettle. He touched the kettle. It was still warm. Someone had been in here and recently. *Where are you, Will?* This was bad. Very bad.

Moving slowly up the hall, he noticed a wet stain on the wall. The drops continued across the floor toward the front room. He touched the stain on the wall then sniffed the liquid staining his fingers. Metallic. It was blood. *Fuck.*

He raced down the hall to the front room and stopped dead in his tracks at the doorway. There he found Will, face down on the floor. A pool of blood had formed at the side of his head. Daniel didn't need to feel for a pulse. He could see what was left of his head and he knew.

* * * *

Beth was just finishing washing the cups and glasses, placing them on the drainer, when Kevin came into the kitchen after making several phone calls in his study.

"You hungry?" he said, as she turned around just in time to see the mischievous twinkle in his eyes.

She couldn't help but smile back. "Not really. Shouldn't we wait for Daniel?"

"Aw, do we have to?"

Beth laughed. "It would be the polite thing to do, wouldn't it?"

Kevin grinned back at her. "Aw, jeez. I suppose we should wait for Danny boy. But he wouldn't mind. He's used to feeding himself." He gestured for her to return to the lounge room.

"So I've noticed," she said, going back into the hallway. "He manages pretty well for a desk jockey."

"He wasn't always a desk jockey, you know." He followed her into the lounge and smiled at her as she sat down on the couch. "He used to be pretty good at fieldwork. In fact, he was one of the best."

"Yeah, he mentioned that he used to have a different job." She moved to the edge of the seat. "So why did he give it up?"

Kevin shifted from one foot to the other and looked out of the window, avoiding her gaze. Taking a deep breath, he turned to her again. "I think that's something you need to ask Daniel."

"I did." She glanced down at her hands, inspecting her nails. "He wouldn't say."

"Then I guess you'll just have to wait until he's ready."

She shifted her gaze to Kevin again. "But you know."

Daniel nodded. "Yeah, I know, but it's not my story to tell. Ask him again when you know him better."

"I don't think I'll be around him long enough to know him better."

Kevin smiled then and peered over his shoulder at her as he made his way to the door. "I wouldn't be so sure of that."

What the heck did he mean by that? She hesitated before following him back to the kitchen. He surely couldn't think there was anything going on with her and Daniel, could he? *Is there something going on? Nah, of course there isn't.* It was just a few kisses. A few hot, fiery melt-your-bones kisses, but still just kisses. That's what Daniel had said anyway. That's what she thought, wasn't it? She couldn't afford to think anything else. She didn't know him well enough and he came from a different world to her.

Hell, what am I doing? It was ridiculous even thinking about this. She was just a job to him—a means to an end. Once they caught whomever it was who shot that man on the train—presumably the same man who was following them—he'd have no reason to hang around. And the sooner the better, so she could get on with her life. Now if she could only forget how devastating his kisses were and stop fantasizing about his body doing amazing things to hers.

As she walked into the lounge, she caught the tail end of Kevin talking to someone on his mobile.

"Fine, we'll be ready, mate. See you soon." He shoved the phone into his jeans pocket.

"Daniel?" she asked expectantly.

"Yep. We need to get ready. Apparently we're moving."

"We're moving? You're coming, too?"

"Seems so." His manner was so matter-of-fact she was left thinking this was all in a day's work for Kevin the spy. Nothing seemed to faze him. Not so her. She had questions — a million of them.

"Why now? We just got here."

"Danny says it's necessary and I believe him. He'll tell us when he gets here. Come on. Let's get this gear of his out to the back lane. He'll be here in a few minutes."

Kevin disappeared into his study and reappeared in a couple of minutes with a backpack of his own. When Beth started lugging the tent bag, Kevin stopped her.

"We won't need that, just the smaller duffel bags. Don't forget your clothes and pretties."

Beth smiled. "Pretties?"

Kevin grinned. "Whatever it is you ladies need for — you know...personal stuff."

"No problem, I haven't even unpacked yet." She smiled to herself. This guy was cute. Not her type, but cute all the same.

It was less than ten minutes later as Beth was waiting behind the gate to the back lane that she heard the car approaching. The laneway was dark and the car's lights were turned off. Beth opened the gate after she saw Daniel through the gap in the fence.

Without stopping to speak, he picked up several bags and headed back to the car. She followed and joined him at the boot. It was a dark station wagon — their third car in four days. This must've been something of a record.

As Beth went back to the yard to collect her last bag, Daniel finally spoke. "Where's Donnelly?"

"He's getting the last bag. He should be here any minute."

"Good, we need to get out of here."

"What happened, Daniel?"

Beth could see Daniel's eyes narrow and his face draw tight. "I'll tell you when I'm sure we're safe."

The sound of the back door closing had them both turning back to the path and at Kevin while he approached. Without speaking, they all got in the car with Daniel driving, Kevin riding shotgun and Beth in the back, resting her leg on the bench seat after she'd clicked on the seat belt.

Kevin glanced over his shoulder. "What's up with the leg?"

"I damaged my knee in the crash. It still gets a little stiff now and then."

"She's had major reconstruction work on it. She should be in rehabilitation."

Beth laughed. "I think it's gotten a lot more exercise these past few days than in a month of rehab. It's moving better than it was before."

"At least you're finding something beneficial in all this excitement," said Kevin.

"Just call me Pollyanna," she answered.

"I hate to interrupt your private joke, but you should really get some sleep, Beth. We have a long night ahead of us."

"Why? Where are we going?" she asked.

"Brisbane."

"Brisbane? That's over a twelve hour drive! We don't have time for that. The Conference is in three days."

"We're not driving all the way. Just go to sleep, and I'll wake you when we get to the next stop."

"Okay, but if we're going to be traveling great distances, we need to eat. Can we stop off at a drive-through? I'm not sleeping until I know you've eaten something."

Kevin coughed, but stopped quickly when Daniel glared at him. Kevin glanced over his shoulder at Beth and winked.

Beth's stomach called again. Loudly.

Daniel snorted. "Okay, you win. Food it is."

Chapter Nine

They stopped off at a burger restaurant a little way before the entrance to the freeway heading north. After ordering enough to feed an army, they took the food back to the car to eat. Daniel raised an eyebrow at the two burgers, large fries and apple pie that Beth had ordered. She'd warned him she ate more when she was stressed, but now she was trying to convince him that she wanted to make sure *he* was fed. Cute.

Sure, that was it. As if she had any reason to care about what he did. Not after the way she'd been lied to, taken on this rollercoaster ride across the country, then to top it off he cops a feel when she slips in the shower. It was a goddamned miracle she hadn't run away from him, or listened to anything he said. Damn, but she certainly filled out that towel well. He felt the blood go south even thinking about it. *Don't even go there, Daniel.*

Nah, she was just trying to hide her amazing appetite from Kevin. She'd become pretty chummy with him in a very short time. And why not? Kevin never had much trouble attracting women. It was the Irish charm and that blarney he came out with. He was such a flirt. But why did it bother him so much? He and Kevin always competed for women. It was a friendly rivalry. All he had to do was tell Kevin to back off and he would. But did he have a right to ask? And if he did, what would Kevin make of it? When this was over, he'd probably never see Beth again, but why did that thought make him feel just a little empty?

"So are you going to tell us what happened?" asked Beth.

Daniel stiffened and took a deep breath. *There is only one way to do this,* he thought. *Just tell her straight.*

"Someone got to Will."

"The helicopter pilot?"

Daniel nodded. "He's dead."

Beth paled. "Who did this?"

"He arranged to get me a car, and before I showed up to collect it, someone shot him."

"Oh God." Beth buried her face in her hands. Daniel fought the urge to jump over the seat and take her in his arms. He settled for reaching over and squeezing her shoulder instead.

"It's not your fault, Beth. You do know that, don't you?"

"I don't know what to think, Daniel. Ever since we've met, I've been followed and shot at and I'm constantly scared. And now someone else has been killed, all because of something I can't even remember. I just don't see a way out of this."

Kevin cleared his throat. "I think this is when I put in my two cents worth. I think I should put you both in an ASIO safe house. I know a place not too far from here. No one in the AFP knows about it."

Daniel shook his head. "No, I don't agree. We need to get to Brisbane and find a place for us without outside help. Somewhere no one knows about. There are obviously some security breaches going on here and I think we'll be safer without anyone knowing—you included, Kevin."

"You don't suspect me?"

"Of course not, but I'm also thinking of your safety. If you don't know, they won't come after you."

"So Kevin's not coming with us?"

"No, I've changed my mind. This is where you get out, mate."

"I understand where you're coming from, Danny boy. You know where to find me if you need anything. I'd better get off the bus then. It's been a pleasure, Beth," said Kevin, as he took her hand and gently kissed her knuckles.

Beth laughed. "Yes, it has been, you flirt you." Her smile faded. "You be careful, Kevin."

"I'm always careful," he said. He opened the car door and jumped out. "Farewell, fair lady."

"Cut it out, Kevin, before I throw up."

Daniel joined Kevin at the boot of the car and handed him his backpack. "I meant it, Kevin. Sorry about the change of plan, but it's safer for all of us this way."

"I know, Danny boy, but if you get stuck, you know where to reach me."

"Yeah, I know."

Daniel watched Kevin walk out of the car park and head for the railway station before he rejoined Beth in the car. She'd moved to the front seat and was stuffing the uneaten food into a paper bag. Her hands shook as she twisted the end of the bag closed before tossing it toward the bin outside the open window, missing it by several inches.

"Damn," she said, grabbing the door handle.

"Leave it."

"I can't leave litter lying around…"

Daniel started the car up and shoved the gearstick into reverse. "Leave it. We haven't got time."

The car roared to life as Daniel reversed and drove out of the car park. He headed down some back streets, avoiding the highway.

"Where are we going?"

"Not Brisbane...yet. We need to stay in Sydney for another day at least to check up on some things."

"Like who killed Will?"

"Among other things."

"So why did you tell Kevin we were going to Brisbane?"

"The less people who know where we are, the better."

Daniel pulled over to the side of the road next to a large wall. The sign indicated a waste management site. The stench of rotting garbage made Beth nauseous and she cupped her hands over her nose.

"Why are we stopping here? This is a rubbish tip."

"Get your bags. We're dumping them."

"Dumping them? Whatever for?"

"Someone knew I was meeting Will. I can't take a chance that there's some sort of tracking or listening device hidden in any of our gear. We'll dump it all here, including the phones. I'll keep the money and we can replace anything we need."

"So you think that's how they keep finding us," said Beth, as she handed Daniel the bags to throw over the wall.

"I don't know, but I can't afford to take the chance."

"So where to now?"

Daniel opened Beth's door for her. "Let's go shopping."

* * * *

The shopping mall was crowded, making it easy for them to blend in with the masses. Loaded up with purchases, they'd changed clothes, including their underwear and shoes, discarding what they'd been wearing. Daniel led them to an electronics shop where they replaced the laptop and bought a couple of prepaid mobile phones. Beth followed Daniel in a daze, still not quite able to take in the fact that Will had been killed. With that public servant on the train and the train driver, that made three people dead. The whole thing was so surreal. This couldn't be happening to her—ordinary Beth Hamilton, receptionist and computer student. It was inconceivable that someone wished her dead. The worst part was not knowing who—never knowing if the person behind her was one of those trying to kill her. Never knowing when they would strike.

Daniel walked beside her with such confidence. He appeared relaxed as he pushed the supermarket trolley he'd commandeered to carry the load of articles they'd bought. They could be any other couple out enjoying shopping together. *How does he do it? How does he live with the constant danger that comes with his choice of job? Oh yes, he doesn't do it anymore. He has a desk job now.*

Now Beth understood a little of why he'd left the field. It must've been so tough living with all that stress on a daily basis. She'd only experienced it for a few days. She couldn't imagine living with it day in and day out.

Daniel's eyes lit up as he stopped and stared at something in the distance.

"Cool. I think it's time for a little indulgence, don't you?"

"Indulgence?"

He laughed as they pulled up to an ice cream vendor.

"Chocolate chip? Or are you a pistachio fan like me?"

"Pistachio? Oh, ice cream. Yes, I love pistachio. Double scoop, waffle cone, thanks."

Daniel chuckled again. "Coming right up. Take a seat. Watch the trolley and I'll be right back."

"So where to now?" asked Beth, when Daniel returned a few minutes later with their ice cream. "I thought we were heading to the Conference? At least, that's what you'd told Kevin."

Beth watched as Daniel licked a small drizzle of ice cream from his fingers. Sudden heat surged through her as she zeroed in on his lips, remembering the feel of them on her own. His eyes met hers as he stopped mid-lick then brought his mouth down and sucked on his fingertips one by one, his eyes never leaving hers. She felt a tingle between her legs and moisture in her panties as she imagined him doing things to her in the same slow rhythm as his finger, moving in and out of his mouth. *Oh God!*

Not now, don't think about it now. She bowed her flushed face, staring at her own fingers and wiped them roughly with a napkin.

Daniel hesitated, winking at her before swallowing the last of the cone. He reached behind him and threw his crumpled napkin in the rubbish bin. When he turned back, he was all business again. "For the time being, we need a place to crash and get on with my computer search. There has to be something we're missing. Someone knew where we were in Canberra and I'm not sure how, but at least now we're clean of possible bugs and if I'm right, we're safe for the time being."

How does he do that? He can turn the heat on and off like a light switch. She needed a minute to cool down so she screwed up her paper towel into a tight ball and stood to walk over to the bin and throw it in.

"You ready then?"

She swallowed, desperately trying to cool her emotions and praying Daniel wouldn't notice anything amiss. "Yeah, I guess. Where are we going again?"

"We'll know when we get there."

"That's comforting to know."

"I haven't decided yet. We'll work it out when we're driving. If we don't know until we get there, at least whoever is following us will have no chance of knowing either."

"You know, in a scary sort of way that actually makes sense to me. I must be catching on to this spy business."

"Don't get too comfortable. It's not the life for someone like you."

"What do you mean 'someone like me'? Didn't I get myself out of trouble in Canberra? I can hack it if you can't."

"Hey, don't jump down my throat and get all defensive. I didn't mean I thought you couldn't hack it, just that a woman like you deserves a normal life with a family and all that goes with it—not a life in the shadows and having to keep secrets from those you care about."

"Don't you deserve that, too?"

Daniel shrugged and stood up. "It's not a priority for me. I have other plans for my life."

Beth followed him as he wheeled the trolley toward the car park. "And that includes being by yourself for the rest of your life?"

"Works for me. Let's get this gear to the car and take off."

Well, that confirmed what she'd originally thought. He was the love 'em and leave 'em type. He did warn her after that spontaneous combustion kiss. Good thing she'd stopped herself from caring too much. *Yeah, good thing all round.*

* * * *

The sleazy hotel they checked into in Kings Cross was a far cry from the five-star luxury of the previous night. The stench of cigarettes and stale beer had Daniel coughing to cover the gag threatening to close over his throat. He didn't want to think how bad this place was and how Beth didn't belong here. If *he* was gagging, what the heck was *she* feeling? After he handed over the cash to the long-haired, scruffy guy who passed as the receptionist, he turned to find her staring out at the street outside. A couple of kids were passing. They couldn't have been more than fifteen or sixteen, but they were dressed to kill in short skirts, high heels and tight tank tops. Heavy eye makeup and lipstick marred their adolescent faces. Such was life in Sydney's notorious Kings Cross, but from the shocked expression on Beth's face, it was something she'd hadn't seen much of in her past, which was amazing since she'd grown up in Sydney.

She turned to face him as he approached. A small tear escaped and trickled down her left cheek before she managed to swipe it with the back of her hand. "They're so young. They should be giggling in the back row of the movies with their boyfriends or having sleepovers with their girlfriends, not walking the streets soliciting paying customers."

Daniel hustled her toward the dingy stairs. "Yeah, well, sometimes life sucks and people are forced to do some crap things to survive. Not our problem at the moment. Let's get to our room so we can get out of sight."

"Don't you care?"

Daniel stopped after he turned the lock in the door to their room. "Once, a long time ago, I thought about how it'd be great to right all the wrongs of the world, but guess what, sweetheart? No matter what we do, there'll always be another street kid turning tricks. It never goes away."

"That's a cynical attitude."

"Yeah, well, I'm a realist. Life seldom turns out the way we'd like it to." He placed his hand in the small of her back and urged her into the room. "Okay, let's get the door closed. The walls have eyes and ears."

* * * *

"Where the hell are they?" the silver-haired man demanded.

"Still in Sydney. I'm closing in on them now. It won't be long and the problem will be eliminated," the man at the end of the phone replied.

"It had better be. You owe me this and you're being paid very well for your trouble. Don't even think of failing."

"Don't worry. This is one assignment I'm going to enjoy."

The silver-haired man grimaced. "You're one sick bastard, you know that."

The other man chuckled. "I'm not the one giving the orders here."

"But I get no pleasure out of this business. If there was any other solution…but there isn't, so get on with it, and don't tell me any of your sick fantasies."

The other man snorted. "Whatever. I'll be in touch." He shut off his phone and whistled as he started up his car and headed into the city.

It won't be long now, he congratulated himself. It was all coming together. Finally.

* * * *

The room was better than Daniel had expected, considering the hygiene level of the lobby. At least the bed appeared to have clean sheets and the small sink on the wall was clean. He couldn't say the same for the moth-eaten carpet though. Beside the bed, there was a large rusty stain that could only be an old blood. He hoped it was from someone's sinus condition and not something more ominous. He dumped the bag over it, hoping to cover it before it got Beth's attention. She was uptight enough just from being in the 'Cross'. She didn't need any more reminders of the seedier side of life. He scanned the room for any more surprises but, finding none, he sat down on the bed and began unlacing his shoes.

"How long do you think we need to stay here, Daniel?"

The first shoe plunked on the floor and Daniel let out a breath. "I'm hoping I'll be able to access more files tonight, and if we're lucky, by tomorrow we might have a better idea who we can trust on this thing. Maybe just one night, two at the most."

Daniel watched Beth as she sat down on the only chair in the room. A throwback from the sixties, the seat was a murky mixture of olive green and orange stripes. Well, it might have been those colors once. Years of sweat and dirt now made the colors merge into one. It didn't seem too sturdy either.

"You sure you want to sit there? There's plenty of room over here."

Beth flushed to the roots of her magnificent red hair and sat down quickly.

"It's okay. I'm sure it'll take my weight." She crossed her shapely legs and placed her hands on either side of her on the seat of the chair, gripping the edges. "I suppose I can handle a couple of nights here. If you think this is safe, I'd stay anywhere."

Daniel smiled. "Even camping?"

Beth laughed, her stiff demeanor relaxing a little. "Well, probably not camping again. You know how well that turned out last time. My dad was right. Camping is bad news."

Daniel watched as she uncrossed and crossed her legs, bringing instantly to mind a scene out of *Basic Instinct*. He shook his head to purge the image of those long, gorgeous pins wrapped around his hips. "We should get some rest. We have a busy day ahead of us. I'll go and get us some takeout then we should try to get some sleep."

Beth stiffened in her chair again although she stayed glued to the seat. The idea of being left alone in this room obviously didn't sit well with her. "Okay, I promise not to open the door for anyone and I won't make any phone calls either."

She looked away as Daniel approached her. He touched the soft skin of her cheek, turning her face to meet his gaze. "Beth, you know it's for your own safety…these precautions?"

Her eyes shimmered with unshed tears. "Yes, I know. I just wish it was over. I want my life back, but whining about it won't help, so you get going and I'll be here waiting."

Shit! He hated to leave her while she was upset, but they had to eat and he would be back in a flash. "You'll be all right?"

"Go!" she said, breaking the contact and pushing him away.

"Okay, I'll be back as soon as I can." Flashing her an encouraging smile, he headed for the door.

"Daniel...?"

He turned back. "Yes?"

"Don't you think you'd be more comfortable with your shoes on?"

Daniel stared at his bare feet and laughed. "I suppose I'd better put them back on. Although bare feet are common in these parts, you never know what might be on the ground."

Minutes later, he was out of the door and Beth found herself alone. She thought back to the other time she'd been alone in a hotel waiting for Daniel to return. She'd been pretty annoyed with him for keeping her out of the loop, and had decided to take matters into her own hands. Fat lot of good that had done. It'd almost gotten them both killed. No way was she moving out of the room this time. She'd learned that lesson the hard way.

She looked around the dingy surroundings and wrinkled her nose. If only they could have stayed five star again. She was in her hometown but she'd never stayed in this part of town before. Sure, she'd driven down Darlinghurst Road with a group of people to check out the scenery, but she'd never really thought about the people who lived there. It was different when she thought of the place as a tourist trap. What she'd seen in the last hour was enough for her to change her opinion completely.

Her mind went back a couple of days to when they'd been in Canberra. Maybe if she went through everything that had happened step by step, she could work out how they'd been discovered, and maybe even who was following them. Images of their arrival in the hotel flashed in front of her eyes. The dinner and what had happened after when she fell in the shower came to mind. *How embarrassing*. Her skin warmed several degrees, her heart pounded and her breathing came in and out in short spurts. Memories of Daniel's firm, demanding lips on hers came back in a rush and she gasped. His unique scent lingered in the room and teased her nostrils and the path his hands had followed now burned with intense heat. Unable to sit still, she stood and paced restlessly around the room.

This was stupid. It was getting her nowhere. She spied the jacket Daniel had left strewn over the bed. She picked it up, pressing it to her face and inhaling, groaning as she breathed in his unique masculine scent.

Oh yeah, she had it bad.

Back to business, Beth. What happened next? She recalled scrolling through the diary on the laptop. She remembered feeling lonely. *Wait,* now she remembered. Her father's friend hadn't answered when she'd attempted to call him. But he couldn't be involved, could he?

A key sounded in the lock and Beth jumped, her heart once again thumping. She moved to the window, not sure what she could do if a stranger accosted her, but there was a small balcony outside where she could escape if she needed to. She grasped the window frame and was poised to force it open if need be when Daniel walked through the door.

"Everything okay?"

Relief flowed through her. "Thank God it's you! You almost gave me a heart attack. How about we come up with a secret knock or something? I almost jumped out the window, you know. I was this close," she said, with her thumb and forefinger placed an inch apart in front of his face. She couldn't stay mad at him and broke into a smile.

Daniel smiled sheepishly as he placed a paper bag down on the small table. "Sorry, I was rushing back to feed you. I know how much you love your food, but you're right, I should have knocked first."

"Well, since you've brought food, I'll forgive you this time." She recognized the aroma of something spicy. Oh yes, just what she needed to banish the thoughts of the last few minutes.

"Is that what I think it is?"

"If you're thinking sub sandwiches, then you'd be correct. They're two doors down. I didn't want to leave you by yourself for too long. I'm glad to see you approve of my choice."

Daniel handed her a sub and napkin and seated himself on the bed before opening his own sandwich.

Beth watched as he took the first bite. He let out a groan of pleasure. Beth's breath hitched and she turned away. Her internal thermostat rose another twenty degrees just thinking about those incredible lips as he tasted her sensitive body parts. Her nipples tightened when the flush expanded to cover her whole body. *Down, girl! Back to business.* She should tell Daniel about what she remembered, and now was as good a time as any. She forced herself to breathe deeper and slower.

"Daniel, I've been thinking."

Daniel polished off the rest of his sandwich in another two bites. "Hang on a sec…"

Beth turned back to him in time to see him place his fingers one by one into his mouth to suck the juices from the sandwich off. She grabbed her bottle of cola and took a large swig, taking in the liquid too quickly and coughing desperately.

Daniel jumped up from the bed and patted her on the back. "You okay?"

Mortified, Beth sucked in a couple of deep breaths and nodded, not trusting her voice at this stage. *Jeepers creepers*, how was she going to get through one night in the same room as him, let alone two? Every movement, every gesture, had her hot, thinking of the things he could do to her body and her to his.

She gradually stopped gagging and she took another sip, carefully this time. "Yeah, I think so. Thanks for the back pat though. I needed that."

"You said you'd been thinking about something, Beth. What was that all about?"

Grateful to move on, Beth took another small sip of her cola before she walked across to the window to stare at the street below.

"I've been trying to piece together everything we'd done and everyone we've spoken to since this started. I thought I could figure out where they picked up on our position, and following on from that possibly who."

"And what did you come up with?"

"I remembered something about what happened in the hotel in Canberra."

"What else happened?"

"When you were out, and before I went out on my adventure, I called a friend of my father who lives in Canberra."

"You *what*?" Daniel jumped up and walked over to her, the sparks from his dark eyes almost touching her skin as he came closer to her.

"I thought it was okay. He worked with my father for years and I hadn't seen him since my parents' funeral."

"Beth...you know I asked you not to call anyone. Why didn't you tell me?"

"I actually forgot about it."

He placed his hand on her shoulder and spun her around to face him, the heat from his touch burning through her shirt. "How could you forget something as significant as this?"

"I'm sorry. I got distracted with running from the bad guys. He wasn't there anyway. I didn't even leave a message. But why would he be after me? He was my father's workmate."

Daniel's hand dropped and he stormed back to the bed, sitting down. "Haven't you learned anything from this, Beth? We can't trust anyone."

"I'm sorry, Daniel. I know better now. I was feeling lonely and wanted to hear a friendly voice. It won't ever happen again." Beth tried hard, but it was difficult to keep the tears out of her voice. She gulped back a sob and started for the bathroom.

"Hell..."

She fumbled for the door and Daniel was there in front of her, pulling her into his arms.

"I've been such an idiot. I should have known better. It was just that I was so lonely and I thought that if I spoke to someone who knew my parents..." A small tear slid down her cheek. *Damn.* She never cried, but in the last two days the tears had been running like a river in flood.

"It's okay," said Daniel as he pulled her even closer and rubbed his hand up and down her back. "Shh...we're in this together."

It felt good. Too good. The heat that was generated was stimulating other parts of her body that had no business being stimulated. From the hardness she felt as she brushed against his jeans, the same thing was happening to him. He tilted her chin and she gazed into his eyes. His face inched closer as his lips descended. With a featherlight touch, he kissed her once, twice, but as he moved in for a closer exploration, Beth placed her hand on his chest, pushing gently, forcing some badly needed distance between them before she found herself melting into him. Daniel dropped his arms to his sides and stepped back, his short, sharp breaths letting her know it was just as difficult for him. She turned her head away from him—his smoldering eyes were too much of a temptation.

She cleared her throat to mask her raspy voice. "It couldn't be Uncle Jack. Someone must have been monitoring his phone. He would never try to hurt me."

"How good a friend was he? When did you last see him?"

"When I was younger, my parents socialized with him and his wife. He frequently came to our home." She took a few steps toward the table, picking up her cola and lifting the bottle up to her mouth, taking a long drink before putting it back down. "The last time I saw him was at my parents' funeral."

"I wish you'd told me about this before, but there's nothing we can do about that now. At least we have another point of entry to investigate. Tell me, where does your uncle work?"

"Some government department in Canberra. I don't think he's ever told me exactly where, and I probably didn't think to ask."

"That doesn't give us much to go on."

"I'm sorry…"

"Forget it. I need to think. I'm going to take a walk. I won't be long. Will you be okay?"

Panic gripped Beth as she sucked in a breath and felt her heart slam in her chest.

"You're not okay..."

She swayed on her feet as she reached behind her back and steadied herself on the table. "I'll be fine. I just need some air. If I put on the wig, can I come with you?"

"I don't think—"

"Please, Daniel... I'll suffocate in here by myself. I'll be careful. I promise. I won't do anything to attract attention. Don't say no."

Daniel stood in front of the door and stopped, his back to her. "The short blonde one. And hurry up. We should get some sleep sometime soon."

Yes! Without waiting for him to change his mind, Beth grabbed the bag of disguises and headed for the bathroom, closing the door firmly behind her.

* * * *

Five minutes later she emerged, transformed. Daniel stared at her. She'd changed clothes. With the spiky-heeled shoes, her legs seemed to go on forever. The short black skirt fit snugly across her mid-thighs and the fabric of the red tank top stretched taut across her breasts. He hardened instantly. *Shit! This is a bad idea.* He tried to turn away, but couldn't. Not until he'd checked out every sexy little inch of her disguise. She'd made up her face and painted her sexy lips with a deep red lipstick. The blonde hair of her wig curled provocatively over her forehead and his hand itched to slip a spiral behind her ear. This was a different Beth to the one he'd come to know. She was more confident somehow. Her eyes were a flash of green light, daring him to challenge her. His gaze traveled from her eyes down her body once more. When he stopped at her breasts, she made a small gasping sound and he saw her nipples outlined through the strained material. They'd better get out of there and fast before he did something stupid, like throw her on the bed and show her exactly how she made his anatomy react. He grabbed her arm and dragged her to the door. "Let's go!"

She stood her ground and shook off his arm. "Do I look okay?"

"Yeah, fine. Let's get out of here."

"Not too much?"

"No. Yes… Maybe. But we'll wing it. Just stick close to me, okay?"

"Okay," she rasped as he once again took hold of her and propelled them into the hall. The door slammed shut as they walked down the staircase. He could feel her trembling under the weight of his hand on her. When they got to the street, he let her go and wrapped his arm over her shoulder.

"What are you doing?"

"Making sure no one propositions you. In that get-up, it's a sure thing."

"Somehow I don't think that was a compliment."

"Take it however you want… Now, let's get that fresh air you wanted."

They moved out onto Macleay Street, into a crowd of people laughing and jostling each other along the pavement. Daniel watched the tourists and locals alike bustling along up and down the main drag of the Cross. Daniel had been there many times, but never with a woman like Beth on his arm. He could feel every leer from every teenager out with his mates searching for fun and every sleazy club bouncer out drumming up business in the many strip joints along the street. His face hurt from the snarls he gave them all. God, she was so damn sexy in that almost outfit. Another big bruiser of a guy stared at her breasts and he had an urge to punch the bozo's lights out. *Jesus*, he'd better get her back to their room soon and pray she'd put on those flannel pajamas she'd bought on their shopping trip that morning. Was it only that morning? Ever since he'd found Will dead, he'd felt as if he was on a treadmill that was gaining in speed. He didn't have the luxury of feeling tired. He'd been living on adrenaline for the last three days and it wasn't going to slow down for a while yet.

Beth shifted position and slid her arm under his jacket to hold him around his waist, her fingers biting into his flesh. He tightened his grip on her shoulders and scanned the area up ahead. A large group of boisterous youths stampeded toward them.

"We'd better get out of their way," said Daniel.

"I agree, but where?"

When the marauding crowd was almost upon them, Daniel pushed Beth through a door that led to a staircase down to a basement. Unfortunately, it appeared that this was the intended destination for the group they were trying to escape from. They were propelled forward by muscle and testosterone into a room at the bottom. Inside they were pushed up against a wall as the rest of the group entered and took their places in a row of seats surrounding a catwalk-style stage. The musky smell of sandalwood permeating the walls was strong as Daniel edged toward the exit with Beth's hand in his. When they neared the door, it was closed by the bouncer they'd seen before on the street. The lights went out and the audience went wild with wolf whistles and cheers.

Daniel leaned over and whispered in Beth's ear. "I guess this means it's show time. We'd better wait for a bit." *God, she smells so good.* He inhaled deeply. Unable to think of one excuse to keep his mouth close to her face, he stood upright again, but not before her gentle shudder.

"Er…show time? Just what kind of 'show' is this?"

"Shh…try to be inconspicuous. We may be able to get through the door unnoticed if we're lucky. Just sit tight through the first act. We'll make a move during the applause."

The spotlight went on as the curtain opened and the music started. Ravel's *Bolero* squeaked and crackled through a sound system that must have predated vinyl records. A young woman with flowing black hair, whose body was draped in magenta gauze veils, swayed to the music as she twirled and stepped her way down the catwalk.

"Oh my God — this is a strip show!"

Daniel's hand came over her mouth and his lips brushed her ear. She could feel his warm breath as he whispered, sending shivers of sensation all over her scalp. "You'll have to lower the decibels if we're going for inconspicuous. If the show's too hot for you, you can always close your eyes."

Close my eyes. Yes, close my eyes. That'll work. I can do this. Bloody hell, I'm watching a sex show with a man who makes me sweat thinking about him!

Closing her eyes wasn't going to fix the problem. And besides, once she spied the girl moving, she couldn't take her eyes off the stage. She inhaled deeply as Daniel withdrew his hand from her mouth. "I'm all right, just a little surprised." She could swear she heard a hint of a chuckle from Daniel as he slid his arm back around her shoulder.

The girl leaned suggestively into the audience. A young patron in the front row took one of her veils between his teeth and drew it off her body.

Beth gasped.

When the crowd caterwauled and several men reached for her, the girl deftly withdrew and blew a kiss to the audience before moving off the catwalk to the stage area where a red velvet lounge chair had appeared. Only a few scraps of material covered her lithe body and what was there left little to the imagination. Her large nipples and areola peeked through the transparent fabric, as did the dark shadow of her pubic hair between her thighs as she swayed to the music. She stopped before the chair, faced the audience, and stood perfectly still. The music stopped and the crowd went wild. Cries of 'Get it off!' and 'Show us the rest!' filled the room. The girl's face was expressionless, but her eyes shimmered with passion while she awaited the next part of the performance.

Beth stood on her toes to whisper in Daniel's ear. "She's getting off on this."

Daniel shifted uncomfortably in place and tilted his head down to answer her. "They aren't all forced in to this life. Some actually do it because they like it."

"I can't imagine wanting to bare yourself to strangers like this."

Daniel shifted again and cleared his throat. "I hear it's a favorite fantasy for some women."

Now it was Beth's turn to be squirm. She didn't want to admit it, but being in this room and thinking about being naked and adored in front of all these men aroused her more than she would ever have thought. Lucky the lights stayed low, she thought as she felt a flush of heat rise over her face and spread through the rest of her body. She licked her dry lips and attempted to answer him, only managing a croaky, "oh". What could she say after that revelation? An image of herself standing naked in front of Daniel flashed through her mind. Her core temperature blasted off the scale when she pictured his eyes glazed with passion for her. *Stop!* With reluctance she turned her attention back to the stage, where a drummer began a pulsating rhythm, the girl swaying to its beat. The spotlight shifted to the side of the stage and a man appeared. He was tall, muscular and gorgeous, and wore tight leather pants with a leather bolero vest. In his right hand he carried a large whip. The handle was thick and black and shaped like a large phallus. He flicked the leather coil toward the audience before aiming at both sides of the girl.

Oh shit! Beth felt for Daniel's hand and squeezed.

The performer raised his hand and Beth held her breath. The room fell into silence. Daniel tightened his grip on her shoulder, sending waves of heat through to her very core.

The first crack of the whip caught Beth's attention, her eyes unblinking as she watched it snake across the woman's breasts, leaving a thin pink slash before removing the offending piece of cloth. Wetness flooded Beth's panties as she swallowed, anticipating the next flick of the whip. It felt as if she was on stage and not the performer.

Crack! Again it flicked out, removing the cloth over the girl's mons. Now the girl was exposed completely. The scent of her arousal assailed Beth's nose, inflaming her growing desire and ramping up her own body's desire to find release from the tortuous tension building inside her. Discreetly she peeked at Daniel, wondering what he thought of this erotic performance.

Out of the corner of her eye she saw him readjust the bulge in his pants and realized she wasn't the only one affected. With the third crack of the whip, her eyes flew back to the stage and she bit back another gasp.

The strips of cloth that had been the girl's only covering now lay in shreds on the floor. The crowd hooted and whistled, but Beth didn't hear a thing except the beat of the drum and her own heartbeat thundering.

The man tossed the whip to the back of the stage, behind the girl. He stood in front of her and slowly circled her naked body while she continued to stand perfectly still, no expression showing on her pale face. The spotlight softened and flames erupted from lanterns surrounding the stage. The smells of sandalwood and patchouli wafted over the room and mixed with the cigarette smoke, creating a thick haze.

He picked her up and laid her down on the lounge chair, posing her with her arms above her head and her legs apart. He stepped back, exposing her body on full display to all. As he leaned over and covered her breasts with his hands, Beth gasped. He explored the girl's body, sliding his fingers up and down, then he moved farther along her body, kissing her mouth before trailing back down to her breasts. The girl moaned as the man continued his exploration with his mouth, finally stopping at her labia. He turned to the audience and smiled as he showed them his tongue. The crowd went wild. Laughing, he turned back to the girl, licking his way through her entrance as she thrashed her head from side to side and cried out her release. He shifted between her parted legs and rubbed against her groin in time to the drums. She arched into his exploring hands as he mimicked entering her.

Beth closed her eyes as a moan escaped from her open mouth. She felt every touch, every lick and every sliding movement as if it was happening to her. Her whole body tingled with heat. She was on fire. *Oh God – I have to get out of here!* She shifted out from under Daniel's arm and tugged his hand. "I have to go… I can't stay and watch any more of this."

She saw Daniel checking out the door and at the bouncer, who was engrossed in watching the couple on stage. "Okay, we'll make our way out slowly, so as not to draw attention."

Luckily most of the patrons were seated, facing the stage, when she and Daniel made a quick, quiet escape out of the door and up the stairs. Once they were back in the street, they ran hand in hand back down the half block to the hotel. Inside the room, Daniel slammed the door shut with his foot. Their hands were still joined when Beth stared up into his face. She trembled. His eyes seared hers with a heat she'd never felt before. She was still caught up in the intoxication of the show and her body moved of its own volition. Daniel shifted closer as she reached up to kiss him. But this was no tentative kiss. It went from zero to a hundred in a millisecond.

Beth opened her mouth to his invasion as he took charge. He'd been holding on by a thread ever since she'd emerged from the bathroom in that amazing disguise, and after that wild show they'd just witnessed, he was at detonation point. He wanted to hold back, but the way she made those erotic little moaning sounds into his mouth, control was a thing of the past. He pushed her up against the wall beside the door, trapping her with the heat of his body. The musky scent of her arousal was heady as she lifted a shapely leg and wrapped it around his thigh. *Holy shit!* He had to have her. *Now.*

He slid his hands underneath her top and skimmed over her silky skin. She shivered at his touch and it fired him further. Moving his hands higher, he was relieved that no bra delayed contact with her enticing breasts. Her moans increased when he scraped his palms over her puckered nipples. He almost lost it right there as he moved his hands to her buttocks and pulled her closer to his erection.

Oh yeah, this is what you do to me.

He pushed the crotch of her panties aside with his fingers and delved into her folds. She was hot, wet and ready. He felt her hand as it scraped over the front of his jeans and unzipped them so fast it sounded as if the denim had ripped. With his free hand, he reached for his pocket and pulled out a condom, ripping the packet open with his teeth. Beth snatched it from his hand and rolled it onto his erection, inch by slow inch, driving him insane with her featherlight touch on his hard cock. He couldn't wait any longer. His body was on fire. He lifted her up to just the right level and she instinctively wrapped her legs around his waist. He ripped the crotch out of her panties before entering her, groaning at the feel of her tight, hot pussy. This was no sweet and romantic lovemaking. It was raw and primal and neither of them could stop.

"Yes… Oh yes…" Beth's moans became shrieks as he pounded in to her once, twice, then some more. Her cries of release set off a mind-blowing climax of his own that went on and on until he felt like he dissolved into liquid onto the floor. He kissed the side of her neck as she nestled her head on his shoulder and sighed. Not wanting to lose contact with her, he tightened his hold as she held onto him, and moved them both to the bed, laying them both down, arms wrapped tightly around her.

Beth lifted her head and pulled off the wig. She ran her fingers through her sweat-streaked hair and tried to move away. Daniel tilted her chin and looked into her eyes.

"Are you okay?"

Beth pushed his hand away and sat up, turning her back to him. "I'm fine."

"Did I hurt you?"

"No." She shuffled her bottom a little bit farther away from him, crossing her arms in front of her. She leaned forward, rocking slightly.

Aw hell! He should have known he was coming on too strong. She obviously wasn't ready for that level of intensity. Intensity? Hell, inferno more like it. He wasn't sure he was okay yet either. Reaching over, he lightly touched her shoulder, careful not to surprise her.

"Beth?"

She shrugged his hand aside and released her arms from their vise-like hold of her middle and let her legs slide to the floor. "I'm all right, okay!"

She shook her head and covered her eyes with her hands. Why on God's earth had she done that? Embarrassment filled her. She'd never lost control like that before. She'd promised herself she wouldn't get any more involved with Daniel, but *holy moley*, it'd been amazing. No one made her tingle all over like that. No one but Daniel. How could she face him now? How could they go back to all business and find whoever was trying to kill them?

The weight of the bed shifted as Daniel sat up and zipped his pants. They'd been so impatient, they were still dressed. Beth's singlet top was all askew, her skirt hiked up to her waist. *Ewww.* She needed a shower, but was reluctant to stand in her current state. She moved her legs back onto the bed, pulled the covers over herself and lay back on the pillow, turning her head away.

"You're not okay, are you? I'm so sorry, Beth. I'm not usually that out of control. My only excuse is that you seemed to want it as much as me. Am I right?"

Beth sighed and turned to look at him. He really did fill out a shirt well, and his penetrating brown eyes were intensely beautiful staring at her, waiting for her response.

"Call it momentary madness? I don't know. I've never been to a strip show before. Do people always react that way to one?"

He reached for her hand and stroked her palm gently with his index finger, sending quivers through her body. "Maybe, but in this case I think it had more to do with how we reacted to each other. That hasn't happened quite that way before. Not to me anyway."

"Oh," she said softly, lowering her gaze to his strong fingers as they continued their lazy exploration of her hand. A small thread of hope wound its way around her heart, but then Daniel pulled his hand away and walked to the other side of the room.

"Let's try to get some perspective here. We're attracted to each other. We like each other, and nature took its course."

The thread fell away as quickly as it had formed, disappointment thudding into her chest. *So nothing has changed.* She bit into her bottom lip to stop it quivering as she waited for the bravado to kick in to defend her fragile feelings. "And it wasn't the first time, so don't beat yourself up about it. We're grown-ups here, no big deal. That's what you mean, right?"

"Not quite. I think we could have something really special going for us, but I think we need to be mindful of the situation we're in. We shouldn't get too involved right now when all our focus should be on finding out who's following us. We can't be distracted. *I* can't be distracted. I can't keep you safe unless I have total concentration."

"So what are you saying…the fun's been had, let's move on?"

"No, I'm saying this was amazing, but we should slow down so we can keep our heads together. After this is over, who knows?"

In other words, he was letting her down easy. Wasn't that the classic line—'now's not the right time'? Okay, so if that was the way he wanted to play it, fine. Beth pulled the sheet up around her body and stood, wrapping it around herself. She needed to get herself together, and she needed some sleep. Tomorrow promised to be another stressful day, trying to get off this wild goose chase and make some progress. Maybe he had a point about not getting distracted. All right then, she'd play it cool.

"Fine. I agree. No more sex until we finish. I can handle that. Now excuse me while I go to the bathroom and get ready for bed—to sleep."

She waddled to the bathroom with as much dignity as she could muster and shut the door. When she emerged some time later dressed in her 'granny' pajamas and with her hair wrapped in a towel, Daniel had gone. A note on the dresser told her he was checking out a lead and for her to get some sleep. *Great. Fat chance.* Especially now she was worried about him being out there on his own. The noise from the street was pretty bad too. She didn't really have a choice though, so she toweled off her hair, climbed between the sheets and rested her head on the pillow. Five minutes later, she slept.

Chapter Ten

Out in the crowded street again, Daniel blended with the tourists. He'd taken one of the baseball caps and pulled it down over his forehead to shield his eyes. He pulled the collar of his jacket up around his neck. Walking with his head bent, he kept his eyes straight, holding the crowd in view. He didn't want any surprises, not when they'd remained undetected since leaving Canberra this morning. *Shit, was it only this morning that we left Canberra?* As days went, this must've gone down as one of the shittiest ones he'd ever experienced, except for Beth. Just thinking her name had his cock hardening all over again. He could still taste her. Getting out of that room and away from her was the only option he'd had. Things were getting too complicated for comfort and he needed the space to get his head together. So did Beth.

Sure, the sex had been great. More than great. It had been so intense he'd nearly lost sight of the big picture. But sex wasn't all that was happening here. He'd better focus solely on the job of protecting her, even if he had to make her hate him. And she might just do that by the time this was over, because he planned to keep her with him twenty-four-seven from now on. Once he got back to the hotel, they'd be joined at the hip. She would hate that but tough shit, she'd just have to live with it.

A small park came into view where there were several benches filled with people sitting down drinking and laughing together. Even though what they were doing was illegal, it was better than having a bunch of druggies shooting up in full view, so Daniel ignored them. He walked past a group of teenagers all wearing the uniform of sports logo pants, black T-shirts and woollen caps. How they tolerated those caps in the December heat was beyond him, but fashion made people do strange things. He thought about those spiky heels Beth wore to the club and how they showed off her amazing legs. Oh yeah, not all fashion was bad.

There was an empty bench at the rear of the park, facing the street. The light above the pathway that led there was out, although it was past four in the morning now and the sky was getting less dark. The glow from the shopfronts in the street made it fairly easy to see anyone who might approach him. He sat down, pulled out his mobile phone and punched in a speed dial number.

"Wyatt, where the fuck have you been?"

Interesting choice of words, considering what he'd just been doing. "Nice speaking to you too, Addison. You're going to have to work on your greetings. You've said the same thing to me every day lately."

"Don't get smart with me, you prick. Do you realize what time it is?"

Late, too damn late. "Yeah, it's about time I had some answers. You got any leads your end?"

"Jesus, Daniel, your timing's impeccable, as usual. Nothing concrete. Will was following up on something, but he's been MIA since this morning…yesterday morning now."

He rubbed his brow with his free hand, dreading what he had to say next. "He's dead."

"What? What the fuck happened?" Daniel moved the phone away from his ear as the decibels increased fifty times over and waited for silence.

"He was getting me a car and we were supposed to meet, but someone got to him first."

"Judas bloody priest! I assume you have a good reason for not calling it in."

"I've been kind of busy making sure no one can track us. I'm calling it in now."

"Where are you?"

There was only one answer he could give. "I can't tell you that."

"Bloody hell, Daniel…you need some backup. At least give me an idea of what area you're in so we have some people on standby should you need them."

And end up dead like Will? No way! "No deal, boss. We don't know who the leak is yet, so it's better if nobody knows. What happened to Will is proof of that. What was he onto, by the way?"

Addison's hesitation was brief, but noticeable. "I'm not sure. He didn't say. He didn't even tell me he was getting you a car. It must have been tracked somehow, otherwise how did someone know where to find him?"

Daniel moved to the far edge of the bench and turned his face to the wall, pretending to inspect the graffiti. "So who had access to that info?"

"No one but you and me officially, but he might have told someone else. Did he have any CIs?"

"I know he had at least one confidential informant, but you know how it is. No one gives away their snitches."

"Yeah, you're right. So that leaves us with zip then. Back to square one."

"Not necessarily. Beth contacted someone when we were in Canberra. No one was home and she didn't leave a message, but it could be how we were made. I need to check it out."

A sharp intake of breath came over the line. "Who did she contact?"

"A friend of her dead father. She calls him Uncle Jack."

Dead space met that announcement.

It was probably a full minute before Addison replied, "Did she say anything else about him?"

"Not much, but I'll be questioning her more. I'm not sure if this is anything, but I'll check it out anyway."

"It's probably nothing. Are you sure you have time for this?"

What was on his boss' mind? Didn't he agree this was a lead? "I don't have much more to go on so I have to start somewhere."

"Okay, but keep me informed. You staying put now?"

Not on your life! "Probably not. Moving around gives us an edge. Staying where we are increases our chances of being found."

"You're still not going to tell me, are you? I could order you to, you know."

"And I'd just have to disregard that one, boss. I'll be in touch."

He pressed the End button and leaned forward, staring at the phone. Something nagged him about that conversation, but he couldn't put his finger on it. Maybe he was just exhausted. Hell, he needed to get some sleep soon or he'd be no use to anyone. Maybe he should go and wake Beth so they could get settled into a new place in plenty of time for him to catch a power nap before his excursion tonight. That phone call had left him jumpy. He probably had no chance of sleep until he nutted it out in his mind. He stood, scanning the area as he rose. The same kids were seated near him, still drinking from their vodka bottles and laughing raucously. One couple had moved to the back wall and were going at it, their hands roaming feverishly, the moans getting louder. How could they be still standing considering the amount of spirits they'd consumed? Shrugging, he walked past them, pulled his cap down further, hunched his shoulders and headed back in the direction of the hotel.

* * * *

There was someone following her. She had to move or they'd catch up. The train carriage was empty as she ran through to the connecting door. Damn, the handle was stuck. Her hands were shaking as she rattled it back and forth and tried again. Nothing. Double damn. She kicked it near the bottom and slammed her fist onto the glass. She heard a click and tried it again. Thank God, it opened. She turned and saw the masked figure getting closer. She banged the door behind her and took off through the next carriage. With any luck the door would give him as much trouble as it had given her, allowing her more time to get away. The next door proved easier, but she wished she'd get to the guard's section soon so she could get them to call the police. Her breathing was getting labored now as she continued to run without stopping. How many more carriages were there? She pushed her hair out of her face and stared along the train to see how far she had to run before she'd get to help. The heavy thud of her heartbeat moved from her chest to her head and back again when a hand reached out and touched her on the shoulder.

Her shrieks woke her as she bolted upright in the bed, grabbing her chest in a vain attempt to calm her thudding heart. She recoiled as she remembered the hand on her shoulder and turned to see if it was there. Nothing. It wasn't real this time.

Shit, shit, shit!

She jumped out of the bed and wrapped her arms around her middle, drawing the flannel tightly against her shivering body as she paced the room.

I'm okay... It was just a dream.

She scurried into the bathroom and turned on the basin tap, shivering as the freezing water touched her skin and droplets fell in a slow stream down from her face to her breasts, causing her nipples to tighten and pucker.

Daniel. Just that one sensation brought back the memories of their explosive sex. Her skin burned with heat that expanded from her core to every sensitive cell in her body. Liquid pooled where she remembered the feel of him slamming inside her. Muscles weakened and she leaned forward to grab the edge of the sink. Throwing her head back, she drew in a deep, cleansing breath. *Get it together, Beth!*

Just what did she want from this relationship? She was tired of the mixed signals. One minute he was colder than an iceberg and the next they were fire, dancing together, getting under each other's skins. He said that getting involved distracted him from doing his job. Maybe that was true, but did he really mean it when he said he'd like to see what happened after it was all over? She wanted to believe that, but her past history with everyone she cared about had made her more gun-shy than most. Could she trust him to stick around? More to the point, did she want to take the chance of hoping for something more, only to be shattered and alone again when he walked away? Her brain said probably not, but a tiny slither of hope in her heart wanted it to be true.

She was pathetic. She knew she should pull back, but in her current situation, she didn't think she had the energy. She needed Daniel's strength. If that meant taking whatever he had to give before it all ended, then so be it. She'd worry about the rest when the time came. She sat on the rickety chair, and remembered something her mother had said when she had been a little girl. *'When the right one comes along, you don't have to think about it. It just knocks you for six and you know nothing is ever going to be the same again.'*

Oh, Mum, why aren't you here now when I need you most? Her eyes stung as she tried to hold back the hot tears filling her eyes as she heard a key turn in the lock.

Daniel was back. She wiped her eyes with the sleeve of her pajama coat and turned away from the door.

Daniel froze as he closed the door. Beth sat stiffly upright on the edge of a chair, her back to him. At least he didn't have to wake her up to get packed. The early morning light reflected on her mass of red curls, giving her an ethereal appearance. He caught a whiff of her scent — spring flowers and woman. He took a tentative step toward her, stopping when he heard a muffled sound coming from her direction.

"Beth?"

She sniffed again and wiped her eyes with her hand. *Fuck.* Another piece of that wall he'd built around his heart began to crumble. *Aw hell…*he couldn't stand the thought that he'd hurt her. She didn't resist as he gently pulled her closer and guided her head to his shoulder, kissing her furrowed brow. She tightened her arms around his waist as her tears fell silently onto his shirt. Her hot breath teased him through the damp material.

"I'm sorry. I'm getting your shirt all wet."

"You have nothing to be sorry about. I'm the one who's sorry."

"No, you don't understand. I was thinking of my mother and how much I miss her. I haven't let myself think about her for ages, but you know, with all that's been happening...I just wish she was here to talk to. She was always great at helping me sort out my problems."

"I'm sorry you're mother isn't here for you, Beth. I can't make you any promises for down the track, but I'm here, in this room with you, right now. You can lean on me all you want."

She looked up at him with her beautiful face. There was gratitude there, but there was also need. She needed him right now and he couldn't—wouldn't—let her down. Damn all the promises he'd made to himself. *Damn them all to hell.* He could no longer fight the feelings he had for her and it frightened the bejesus out of him.

They could move locations later. Another hour wouldn't matter.

He lowered his face to hers and brushed her soft lips with his. His erection was instantaneous and pressed painfully against his jeans. He wanted to keep control. He wanted to make this slow and tender, to give her pleasure so she could forget for a short time the crap they were going through. He shifted his body backward slightly so there was no contact other than his hands on her shoulders and his lips on hers, kissing her as if she was a fragile piece of porcelain.

Beth shook from the sweetness of his kiss. Her body reacted in every pore as goosebumps appeared, sending tingling sensations from the outside in. Now she knew what people meant when they described a visceral reaction. Every cell in her body clenched with need as she anticipated the feel of Daniel's graceful hands and his magic mouth. She sighed in contentment as he lifted her in his arms and carried her to the bed. He laid her gently down, not once breaking contact with her mouth. His kisses were intoxicating. The rush of endorphins so intense, the heat from her core spread to the top of her scalp. She would die if he didn't touch her soon. Her breasts swelled and heaved as her nipples tightened painfully when she moved her legs together, rubbing against all of her sensitive areas. She arched her back, showing Daniel exactly what she wanted. She pulled away and placed her tongue in his ear, blowing her breath inside as she pleaded. "Please, Daniel... Please..."

Daniel muffled a groan. "Beth, you're not playing fair. Let's do this slowly. I promise it will be good. I want to give you pleasure."

"You *are* giving me pleasure, but since you asked, I'll wait...for now. You're killing me, and when I can't take any more, I intend to fight back."

Daniel lightly skimmed his finger down the line of buttons on her pajama top. "Don't worry, sweetheart. I'll be ready for you. If your bones don't melt first."

At that gentle warning, Beth's breathing hitched in an erratic frenzy. Anticipation grew as she waited for his next move. She didn't have to wait long. He leaned forward once more and slid his fingers inside the elastic of her pajama pants. Before her next breath he'd removed the offending clothing with one swift movement and thrown them aside.

"Close your eyes and just feel..." he whispered.

"Daniel..." she pleaded.

He placed a finger over her swollen and sensitized lips. "Shh…no talking, either."

She complied with a shudder as he removed his hand. She shivered when a rush of cool air from the overhead fan floated over her bare legs. She held her breath when he placed his mouth on her buttons, undoing them one by one with his teeth. The heat from his breath seared her skin, even though he kept his mouth inches away from her burning skin, driving her crazy with need. He tugged on the sides of her top, sliding them apart to bare her body to him. She arched her back once more and lifted her hips off the bed, sighing. He groaned.

"So beautiful…"

"Daniel…"

"Tell me what you want."

"You told me not to talk."

"I've changed my mind. Don't forget to keep your eyes closed, but tell me your fantasies—what you makes you wet, what makes you shout and scream and lose control. It's all a part of the pleasure."

"Oh…I…"

He blew softly on one nipple. She didn't think it could get any more erect, but she was wrong.

"Do you like that?"

"Ah…"

He blew on her other nipple and she sighed, aching with the need for him to be inside her.

"I guess you do," he murmured, continuing the southward exploration of her body. She parted her legs when the heat reached her labia. He blew once along the length of her folds and she nearly bucked off the bed.

"Careful… I don't want to tie you up…" He chuckled. "But then again, maybe that's one of your fantasies?"

She nearly came right there at the notion of her body restrained, unable to move and open to him — of being used as his personal sex slave. *Oh God! When did I get so kinky?*

"I thought you wanted me to tell you?"

"Mmm…go ahead," he said as he nuzzled her clitoris with his nose, inhaling deeply before swiping across her folds with his clever tongue.

"Daniel…" There was no breath left in her lungs.

"Yes?"

"I want…"

His wet and warm tongue continued its journey, he kissed and licked her skin down one leg to a sensitive patch behind her knee. "Yes…?"

She forced herself to breathe, amazed that she remembered how. "I want you!"

He lifted his head and met her eyes as she opened her lids. He smiled. "Not so fast, my love. All in good time."

"Any more good time and I'll explode." She sat up and reached for him, searching for his mouth. "I'm sorry, Daniel, but I can't wait." She kissed him passionately.

Fire ignited as their mouths touched. He ran his tongue across her bottom lip, teasing her and inviting her to open for him. Invading her sweet warmth, he explored every crevice before thrusting in and out, simulating the dance she was burning for.

They lay back on the bed as the kiss continued. Daniel moved his hands upward to her breasts and squeezed gently. He skimmed his palms over her nipples, setting off a deep moan as she marveled at the sensations he created. He answered her with a primitive growl and he raised his body above hers. His cock gently rubbed against her entrance and slipped inside her, filling her completely.

He started moving slowly in…and…out, each time filling her more as her muscles clenched around his shaft, keeping him buried deep within her for just a second more each time. The tempo increased, and she could have sworn they were both floating above the bed. Her cries of ecstasy came loud and fast as she came apart in his arms. Wave after wave of sensation poured through her as he followed her to the final thrust. They collapsed together and he wrapped her in his arms, where she fell into a dreamless sleep for the first time since she'd woken up after the train crash.

* * * *

Daniel woke Beth a couple of hours later after packing up their gear and scouting the Yellow Pages for possible alternative locations. He hadn't been able to sleep, but he hadn't the heart to wake her before this. She slept so peacefully, with a damn sexy smile playing on her lips. It took all his control not to throw her on her back and screw her brains out again and again, but he'd already gone too far. He needed to switch the emotion chip off for now and keeping his hands to himself played a big part in the success of that operation. *Fuck*. It was bloody difficult, especially when she made those cute sighing noises when she stretched her long arms above her body. *Shit*. He shook his head. *Fucking impossible*.

Luckily Beth flew through her shower routine quickly, and they started on their way without further delay. They ended up leaving later than he'd planned originally, but time enough for him to get some sleep before the action started.

* * * *

The traffic across the Harbour Bridge was busy as usual, with the wire mesh fence obscuring the view of Circular Quay and The Rocks on the left and the coat hanger blocking the sight of the Opera House on the right. The mad scramble across lanes on the north side was no different to any other trip. But this trip wasn't ordinary. The silence between them was a living thing. It grew more intense, thickening the atmosphere the longer they were in the car, with neither of them meeting each other's eyes as the traffic whizzed by. Daniel tapped his fingers on the steering wheel in time to the radio. It was late morning now and they had several hours to fill until he searched the offices tonight. He could think of lots of ways to fill in time, but unfortunately he needed rest more. If he couldn't focus, he would be no good to either of them. Beth fidgeted in her seat and tilted her head upward, inspecting the roof of the car.

"Okay, so where are we going? I hope it's not my place, because it's a mess."

Daniel suppressed a smile and kept his eyes on the road while he picked a brochure out of his pocket and threw it in her general direction. It was for a motel in Chatswood—one aimed at businessmen, offering Internet connections and a business center.

"All right. Another motel. So the plan for the rest of the day is?"

"Sleep."

"Sleep? I can see you need some, but the Conference is only days away. Maybe I can do some snooping around?"

"I'm not convinced this is about the Conference. I think it's more about you and what you saw on the train. Your father's death is connected somehow. I don't know how, but my gut feeling is that the Conference is just a distraction to throw us off track from the real issue."

"Which is?"

"You saw someone on that train, someone who didn't want to be seen. I just haven't worked out how it ties into your father and his friend, but I will."

"You're betting a lot on gut feeling. Are you sure about this? I can't believe Uncle Jack or my father have anything to do with what's happening."

Daniel turned off the highway as they approached Chatswood and its myriad of office blocks. "I want to talk to you more about your father and your Uncle Jack. But I've been running on adrenaline for the last few days, and I need some sleep. It may not tell us anything, but we've got to get farther than we are now."

"I'll tell you everything I know if it will help. And I can help tonight, too."

Daniel smiled at her then. "I know you can, Beth, but we'll talk about that later. For now, let's get some rest."

Daniel steered into the car park of the motel. It was a two story building with access via an internal staircase. The crisp, clean façade indicated a recent renovation. The design was a throwback to the seventies, with terracotta and semi-circular arches everywhere, but it would do for their purposes. He parked the car behind the main building and opened his door. "I'll just be a minute. I phoned ahead and booked, so I just need to sign the registration and pick up the key." He handed her the mobile phone. "Call me if you see anything strange. The keys are still in the ignition. Drive away as fast as you can if anyone suspicious approaches you."

Beth clutched the phone in her hand, her fingers squeezing hard. "Do you think we were followed?"

"I didn't see anyone, but we can't afford to let down our guard."

She tightened her grip even further, her knuckles now white. Daniel smiled at her again and winked. "I'm sure we'll be okay here. I'm just being cautious. Don't worry, Beth. We'll be fine."

"Okay, but hurry back."

"I'll be back before you know it."

"I'll be here."

* * * *

What could she say about the room, other than it was a palace compared to last night's dumpy surroundings. She sank onto the soft bed and lay back on the quilted spread. She inhaled the scent of clean sheets and smiled. Yes, this was much better. Funny how she'd taken the creature comforts for granted. These past few days she'd seen a few, but she'd done without them as well, and she knew which way she preferred it. *No, ma'am, no more camping and no more sleazy hotels in the Cross.* Thinking about the Cross reminded her that it hadn't been all bad. They'd really burned up the sheets, but that was more to do with the heat of the moment than the ambience of the surroundings. She smiled wistfully. She wasn't counting on it happening again in the near future. Daniel had barely spoken to her all morning, and even though on the surface he seemed the same, she sensed that he'd pulled back from her somehow. He was as considerate and as caring as usual, but it wasn't the passionate man of last night who was in the bathroom next door washing up. This man was cool as a cucumber. All business. What did she expect? She'd warned herself that he was just doing a job and not to care too much. Lucky she hadn't gone the whole hog and fallen in love with him — yet.

Daniel walked out of the bathroom dressed in only a pair of silky boxers. His chest was magnificent and Beth couldn't help but ogle. He was drying his hair with a towel when he sat down next to her on the bed. He smelled of spice and pine, and man, and she could feel the heat radiating from his body. She grabbed the edges of the quilt beneath her hands and squeezed hard. He wasn't making this easy.

He dropped his arms and tilted his face toward her, folding the towel as he spoke. "I want you to promise me you won't leave the room while I'm asleep."

"But…"

"No buts, Beth…promise me. If you leave this hotel, you put yourself in danger, and you know that. So what's it to be?"

"You can't expect me to stay cooped up here all day while you sleep."

"It won't be all day, just a few hours. Be reasonable, Beth."

"What if I want to go see a movie? I'll put on my disguise…"

"No way are you putting that outfit on again."

She shivered as she remembered the one he was referring to. "Not *that* disguise. I can fix up another one."

"You can't leave the room. I won't have you out of my sight."

"You won't? How are you going to stop me?"

"If I have to, I'll tie you up."

"You wouldn't!" She blushed at the possibilities that scenario evoked.

"You'd be surprised what I might do."

"Why don't you want me out of your sight? You know I'll be careful."

"You're my responsibility and I need to make sure you'll be okay."

"There's more, isn't there? You're being overprotective for a reason. What is it?" A memory of a conversation she'd had with Kevin came back to her. She moved around to his side of the bed and faced him. "Is this anything to do with why you gave up fieldwork?"

His head popped up and his face flushed red. "Who told you that?" He shook his head. "Fucking Kevin. He had no right!"

Beth flinched, shuffling to the end of the bed, her back to Daniel. "Kevin mentioned there was an incident that was the catalyst for you taking the desk job. He said you would tell me if you wanted me to know. Obviously you don't want to tell me. I'm sorry I brought it up. I was just trying to understand your motives here. I won't mention it again."

"Aw shit!" He stood beside her and touched her arm. "It's not you. I don't talk about this with anyone. I'm not trying to shut you out. It's a painful time in my life and I'd just as soon forget it."

His eyes were bloodshot and his eyelids drooped slightly from lack of sleep. She covered his hand with hers. "It's okay. You don't have to tell me. We hardly know each other anyway."

He turned her hand over and gently squeezed it. "I think we know each other pretty well, actually."

Beth felt herself flush from head to toe. "Mmm...well, yeah, we *know* each other...in the biblical sense..."

"That's not what I meant, Beth. You mean a lot to me. I care about you."

"But you don't trust me yet, and at the moment, we both really need to trust each other. Our lives depend on that." She pulled her hand away and started walking

"Damn it, Beth, you know I care about you."

She saw his pain-filled eyes. He blew out a breath and covered his face with his hands.

"Someone got killed because I didn't do my job properly. Someone I cared about."

She stepped toward him, itching to embrace him and take some of his pain, but he held himself stiffly, forming an invisible barrier that stopped her in her tracks. "Oh God, Daniel. I had no idea."

"Of course you didn't. I didn't tell you. I don't tell anyone."

"What happened?"

"Her name was Lisa. I was assigned to protect her. She was going to testify against her former boss. He was involved in organized crime. We became close. I was distracted and they got to her. End of story."

That explains a lot. Poor Daniel. Her heart ached as she thought about the guilt he must be living with, but he shouldn't blame himself. She closed the distance between them and wrapped her arms around him, hoping he could feel how much it meant to her that he'd finally shared with her. "You know it wasn't your fault. You couldn't have predicted that would happen."

"I'm not so sure about that. If I hadn't been so wrapped up in her, I might have been able to save her."

"That's not the Daniel Wyatt I've seen. You're focused, and you're efficient...but you still care. You can't make me believe it was your fault, but I know you don't want to talk about it now. I'm glad you told me. It makes it clearer why you want us to stay together. I'll try to do what you ask of me until this is over, but I can't promise I'll always agree."

He held her tightly, leaving a featherlight kiss on the top of her head. "At least promise me you'll stay in the room while I sleep. It's important, Beth."

She thought about it for a few seconds then answered him. "Okay, I promise. But I want to have access to the laptop so I can at least do some research."

He smiled as he released her and pulled down the covers. "Fine. But no hacking."

She straightened up. "I know what I'm doing. You've seen my work."

"I know you're good, but I don't want to take the chance. Look what happened in Canberra."

"I outwitted the bad guys and we escaped?"

"I'm serious, Beth. We don't know for sure if it was the phone call or the computer that led them to us, and until we do, I don't want to take any chances."

"I remember your back door. I thought I'd have another gander at Peter's appointment diary. I promise I won't go into the NCA files."

Daniel raised his eyes to the ceiling and took a deep breath. Letting it out slowly, he lay down on his side and dragged the covers up over his shoulders. "I know I'm going to regret this, but okay. Check out his Outlook appointments, but nothing more, all right?"

She squealed in delight and threw herself over him and hugged him tightly. "Thanks, Daniel. Your trust means more than you know."

He laughed. "Hey, I could do with a little air here."

She stood back "Sorry. Now you go to sleep and don't worry about a thing."

"Why am I not comforted by that statement?"

She slapped his ass through the bed covers. "Ha! You'll keep."

"Is that a promise?" His brown eyes were full of heat as he peered over the blankets.

She could feel the embarrassment starting again. This was ridiculous. They knew each other's bodies particularly well by now. She should've been way past embarrassment but no...she still blushed at the slightest hint of anything sexual. No more. She'd face this head-on. She flashed him her sassiest smile, then ran her tongue along her bottom lip provocatively. "Oh yeah. You'd better rest up. You're going to need your strength for later."

Daily sex on demand. Sounds good to me.

She heard a muffled groan as he pulled the covers farther over his head. Cool. *Have pleasant dreams, Daniel!* Chuckling to herself, she walked over to the desk and set up the laptop, the wireless Internet connection a particular bonus. She wanted one when this was all over. If it ever ended, that was.

* * * *

After nearly two hours painstakingly checking over the previous year of appointments, Beth was exhausted. A slight ache had begun behind her eyes and she rubbed her forehead with her fingers to ease some of the tension.

Zip, zilch, nada—nothing had shown up. Nothing that made sense anyway. There were several regular appointments with people only identified by initials. One set more than the others—T.B. There was another couple with T.I. and a couple of times the meeting content was listed as B.H., T.B. and T.I. which meant nothing to her, but B.H. had been her father's initials— Brian Hamilton. Could there be a connection? And who the hell were T.B. and T.I.? She massaged her neck and leaned back in the chair. Were they ever going to figure this out?

A pair of hands touched her shoulders and she nearly jumped off the chair. A warm breath whispered in her ear and set the goosebumps rising all over her body. "Relax. It's only me." Daniel massaged her tense muscles with an expertise that told of years of practice.

She groaned with pleasure as she slowly lowered her head to give him better access. Tingles spread over her skin. "Ah...that feels wonderful. Oh yeah...yes, right there. Oooh, that's good. Keep it up and I'll put you on my payroll."

"It'll cost you. My services are in great demand."

She smiled up at him and winked. "Oh, I think you'll be satisfied."

Abruptly Daniel removed his fingers and crouched beside Beth to check out the laptop screen. "So what have you got?"

All business again. Okay, she could play it that way too.

"A series of initials with no explanations as to what or who they are. But they do occur with regularity."

"T.B., T.I. and B.H. Do they mean anything to you?"

"Only B.H. Those are my father's initials."

"That's not much to go on," Daniel sighed. "I guess we go with Plan B then."

"Plan B?"

Daniel flicked his index finger across the tip of his nose. "Honey, hold on to your hat. We're in for a bumpy night."

"You're mixing up your movie quotes, Daniel. What the heck are you talking about?"

"What I'm saying is — Tonight we go and search Peter Wilson's files."

"Hack in, you mean?"

"No. We break in to his office."

Chapter Eleven

They parked the car a block away from the government offices. Beth sat in the driver's seat, gripping the steering wheel as if her life depended on it. Maybe it did, thought Daniel. If he got caught inside the building, she'd need to drive like a bat out of hell to get away, and he wanted to make sure she was ready for it. He'd instructed her to wait thirty minutes then leave. No exceptions. She was still sulking but she'd finally agreed, only because they'd made arrangements to meet at a place outside the city if they got separated. She'd better not be humoring him. He'd meant it when he told her to drive off without him. It wasn't safe for her to hang around if he didn't make it out. Until they knew who was after them, he was taking no chances.

He leaned over the seat to the back and picked up a small backpack. Opening it, he pulled out a flashlight and placed it in his pocket. Next he pulled a black flannel balaclava over his head then turned to face Beth. Her face was pale in the moonlight, her eyes indistinguishable from the peak of the baseball cap she'd worn to cover up her fiery hair.

"Thirty minutes, okay? Then drive off."

"I'm not happy about it, and if it's twenty-nine minutes and I see you coming down the street, I'm waiting for you, okay?"

"Beth..." He reached for her arm, but she pulled away.

"Just go and do your spy stuff. I'll be all right."

He moved closer to her and framed her face with his hands, preventing her escape. He covered her mouth in a fierce, burning kiss that was over almost before it began. "I know what I'm doing, Beth. I'll be in and out of the building before you know it."

The street was dark and deserted, but Daniel didn't want to take any chances, so he inched his way toward the government building in the shadows to avoid being detected. Almost at the front entrance, he hung back momentarily to retrieve an instrument from the backpack. He attached the small box to the bottom of the door and pressed a button. A red light flashed, beeped and changed to green. The lock clicked as the alarms and locking mechanism disengaged. Sometimes he loved the gadgets that came with his job!

He found the lobby empty. From his research that afternoon, he knew it was the security guards' change of shift. He had five minutes tops to get through the foyer and up to Peter Wilson's office. One last scan of the area and he pushed the fire door open and slipped through. He peeled a pre-cut piece of tape from his wrist and placed it over the sensors on the jamb, silently closing it before moving to the fire escape. He repeated the process again and made his way up the stairs to the third floor.

So far so good.

His luck continued when he found the corridor deserted as he exited the stairwell. He proceeded down the hall silently, stopping halfway when the sound of talking reached him. He ducked into the office on his left side and closed the door.

He held his breath as the two security guards made their rounds. Lucky for him they weren't thorough, choosing not to search the room he was hiding in. He checked his watch. Time was something he didn't have, so as soon as their voices receded, he continued down the corridor to the office he knew from floor plans to be the one Peter Wilson had used. He locked the door behind him and quickly found the cubicle. It was clean. Not one file or scrap of paper remained, let alone the computer terminal. *Fuck! Of course it would be clean.* The files he'd hacked into were on the department intranet. Thank God for slack IT departments. But damn, where else could the physical files be? Destroyed? He hoped not. He left the room and headed back to the stairwell.

* * * *

Beth stared at her watch again. *Damn*, it had been only five minutes since the last time she'd checked. Daniel still had twenty minutes to go. She pulled her jacket closer across her chest and shivered. *He'd better be okay, the idiot.* She knew they had to do this, but the temptation to run away to a desert island and leave this all behind them was a pretty damned good option about now. She peered at her watch again. Bummer, not even a minute. Crossing her arms, she willed some warmth into her chilled body. The street where she'd parked continued to be deserted and the road shimmered with water. Since it hadn't rained all week, it probably came from a street cleaner's truck. The night was clear, but the stars were hard to pick out through the glow from the city lights. She could only imagine where they were as she scanned at the night sky to stop herself checking her watch again.

The door of the car wrenched open and a hood came down over her head, blocking her vision. *Holy shit!* She attempted to pull it off as gloved hands grabbed her own and she heard the zip of tape being unrolled, felt it wrapped tightly around her wrists in front of her.

"What are you doing? Let me go!"

Her assailant remained silent, but she caught a whiff of expensive aftershave as strong arms yanked her to her feet and pulled her a short distance away. Her assailant pushed her forward and she stumbled, hitting her shins against something hard before falling forward into what felt like the back of a van or a utility truck. Before she had a chance to right herself, a door slammed behind her and the engine started. She slipped across the floor with the momentum of the van as it screeched along the street.

Oh God! Calm down and think. She had to get away, but from whom? Who was this guy and how the hell did he find her?

"Who are you?"

No answer. The van swerved around a corner and she slid toward the front of the van, banging her head against the seat.

"What? Too much of a coward to show your face?"

She heard a chuckle from the front seat. She'd heard that laugh before. *Oh no…it couldn't be…*

* * * *

Daniel rifled through the archive boxes in the storage room of the building's basement. It was sheer luck he'd found it. Checking the computer database had turned up nothing. He figured that staff were slow catching up on work everywhere, and took a chance that boxes for archiving would be in a holding area waiting their turn. He'd lucked out. The box in front of him contained the personal effects of Peter Wilson. On the surface it had appeared to be a load of junk, but a framed photo had revealed some ripped pages hidden behind the picture. He hadn't had a good look at them yet. They could wait until he finished checking everything else. He glanced at his watch. Shit, he had less than ten minutes before Beth was supposed to leave without him. He'd better get a move on. Skimming the papers he'd placed on the desk, he saw something that made the hairs on his neck stand up — two names and a nickname — Brian Hamilton, John Addison and 'The Irishman'.

Shit! Beth was in danger! He pulled out his mobile and called her number. It rang out. *Fuck!*

He abandoned the box and ran out of the basement and up the stairs to the lobby. He didn't care if he was seen. He had to get to Beth. Running down the street, he heard the sound of screeching tires where a van turned the corner and drove away at breakneck speed. The door to the car was open and there was no sign of Beth. In seconds he had the car started and followed the direction of the van, but to no avail. He'd lost him already. He pulled over and slammed his fists against the wheel. *Fucking hell!* Beth was gone and he knew who was behind it. He'd been betrayed by everyone he trusted, and he had no idea where to start looking for her.

* * * *

"Kevin?"

The van swerved and stopped. A hand grabbed the hood and yanked it off. The baseball cap fell away as she shook her head to get her hair out of her eyes. When her vision cleared, Daniel's childhood friend sneered. Gone were the cheeky grin and the flirty eyes. Instead he leered at her, his eyes staring at her breasts stretched tightly against the T-shirt where the jacket was gaping.

"I can see now what got Daniel all fired up."

She shivered with revulsion. How in hell had she thought she'd liked this man?

"Why are you doing this? I thought you and Daniel were friends?"

"I'm doing this for the age-old reason, my love. Money. Getting to have some fun with Daniel? Well, that's a bonus."

"You must really hate Daniel. What did he ever do to you?"

"Hate? That's such a strong word. It implies all sorts of emotions I'm sure I don't have." He turned away from her and grabbed a bottle of water from the seat next to him, taking a sip.

"So why are you really doing this?" She scanned the interior of van while she kept him talking. There had to be a way to escape.

"It's all about winning, Beth, my love. For most of my life, I've come second to Daniel. He beat me in exams. He beat me in rugby. He even got a higher security level job than me. But this time I've outsmarted him. He doesn't realize it, but I've been calling the shots for a while now, and there's not a thing he can do about it."

"Who's paying you? Is it terrorists?"

Kevin snorted and started choking on his drink. He slapped his chest through the coughs until they settled down. "Ah, that's funny. No, not terrorists, sweetie. Worse than that. But I'll leave that titbit for when Daniel joins us. I can't wait to see his face when he finds out who's behind this."

Beth shuddered. So much resentment and hate. How had Kevin managed to hide it from Daniel for so long? Daniel would be devastated when he realized it was Kevin all along—another reason to blame himself for what was happening to her. She thought of Lisa and she knew she had to get out of this. Not only for her own sake, but for Daniel's. It would destroy him to fail again. She shifted in place and felt something sharp underneath her thigh, pricking her though the material of her jeans. She saw a lump under a rough scrap of old carpet that doubled as a small mat across the back of the van. She needed to keep him talking for longer. "So why did you let us go when we were at your place?"

He laughed. "Oh, that would have been too easy. This way I get to play."

"What do you mean 'play'?" She grabbed the edge of the carpet with her foot and inched it over to the side. If she could keep him occupied for a bit longer, she might get to see whatever the object was. It was sharp, so she might be able to use it.

"Ah Beth. I could have killed you both, but this way I get to see Daniel squirm first and to see him realize that this time I've outsmarted him. This time *I* win!" He twisted back to her and she stopped moving. His eyes gleamed and his smile was anything but friendly.

"Enough chit-chat. We have places to be, people to beat." He turned the key in the ignition and revved the engine.

"Where are we going?"

"You'll find out soon enough. I'll be calling Daniel to join us, so you might want to conserve your strength. Oh wait…what for?" He laughed as he accelerated down the road.

As soon as Kevin was busy driving again, Beth resumed her fidgeting to uncover the sharp object. She hoped it was something more than a small rock. She had to get away from this madman. A few more inches and she'd have her prize. She slipped her big toe under the lip of the carpet now and bent her knee, pulling the carpet up with her foot. Shuffling her bottom to the side, she looked down. *Glass!* She thanked the fates when she spied the jagged piece of broken glass. No wonder it felt sharp. Now if she could only pick it up... The van drove over a bump and she lifted and fell back down. The glass slid across the floor to the other side, out of her reach. *Shit!*

She threw her body across to the other side where it had fallen, hitting her head on the hard floor and bumping her shoulder on the side wall in the process. Her body would be so black and blue after this. Not that that mattered if she couldn't get away. She'd be dead if she didn't succeed.

Kevin turned his head at the ruckus she'd made and chuckled. "Sorry about the rough ride, my love. But I suppose you're used to the rough treatment with Daniel. Now me? I try to be gentle. Maybe I can show you what I mean, so you can see that Danny boy comes second in that department as well."

Her face flushed with heat and her stomach lurched in revulsion with the thought of his hands on her body. "I'll never let you touch me."

He chuckled. "Aw c'mon. Don't be like that. I know you weren't so shy with Danny."

"Daniel is just protecting me. Nothing else."

"Yeah right, and I'm the King of Bulgaria. Jesus, Beth, the man's in love with you. Even *I* see that."

Beth's heart leaped. Was he right? She knew Daniel cared for her, but love? *No, Kevin's just stirring up my emotions. Just playing another of his games.* "Don't be ridiculous. He's helping to keep me safe."

"Not doing such a good job now, is he?"

"We were doing fine, but you don't play fair. How *did* you find me anyway?"

"I never lost you, sweetie. I put a GPS transponder in the car before you dropped me off. I've been following you ever since. Great strip show, by the way. Did it make you as hot as it did me?"

Oh God! He'd been with them all the time. Why did he let them go for so long?

"You're sick!"

"Yeah…ain't it fun?"

What was the point of arguing with him? With his bent logic, she had no chance of getting anywhere. She closed her eyes and hoped he'd ignore her for the time being. Her hands were now in front of her face and she could see the glass inches away. She slowly lifted her strapped wrists over the shard and manipulated her fingers until she had a grip. She hoped to God that Kevin didn't turn around again anytime soon. She angling the jagged piece toward the duct tape and started slicing.

* * * *

Daniel angled the car into the driveway and jumped out. He raced up the steps and pressed down hard on the call bell. When no one answered, he picked up the heavy knocker and threw it against the plate, the rusty metal vibrating with the echoing noise. The sound of footsteps stopped him from doing it again and he tensed for what he had to say when the heavy oak door opened.

Disappointment filled him when the housekeeper peered through at him, the safety chain still attached.

"Yes?"

He smiled at her. "I need to see Mr. Addison straight away."

"He's not here. He's still at his Canberra residence."

"Are you expecting him this weekend?"

"I'm not sure. He's usually here by now, but he must have been held up. Can I take a message?"

"No, but thanks anyway. I must have been mistaken. I thought we were meant to meet this morning. I'll check my diary."

She closed the door and Daniel walked back to his car. He looked up at the upstairs windows. *Was that moving curtain a person or just the wind?* Not much he could do about it. If Addison was at home, he was avoiding him. He pulled out his mobile and tried Addison's number. Damn, he still had his phone turned off. Where was he hiding?

He drove off, heading toward Balmain. Maybe he could get some answers out of Kevin. He leaned forward, opened the glove box and pulled out the Glock he'd retrieved from his gear. He hadn't told Beth about the gun. He hadn't wanted to scare her. Hell, he never wanted to actually use it, but now he didn't have a choice, not if he was going to get himself and Beth out of this alive. He concentrated on pushing his feelings for her aside so he could work through this like the professional he was, but it wasn't happening. He was angry and scared for Beth, but he was mainly angry. People he thought he'd known as well as himself were now strangers to him. Was his whole life a lie? And Beth? Her father had been involved in an operation that had gotten him and her mother killed. She must have somehow stumbled onto some information that threatened to expose Addison. He now had no doubt that Addison was behind all of this, and he was going to make damn sure the bastard paid for what he'd done. The problem was, where did he start?

Driving into Balmain's narrow streets on a Saturday was a difficult prospect. In a suburb where there was a pub on every corner, parking spaces were at a premium, and Kevin's house was no exception. Opting to take his chances in the rear lane, he pulled up in front of the back entrance. He had walked halfway to the back door when his phone rang.

* * * *

Yes! Her hands were free. The glass had worked its magic and now the duct tape was split up the middle, effectively freeing her. She didn't dare remove the tape for fear of making a sound that would attract Kevin's attention. If she was careful and she kept her hands together, he wouldn't notice right away. She might get lucky and have an opportunity to escape. She was feeling a little more optimistic now. She *would* get away. She had to.

"You doing all right back there, Beth?"

She jumped and clasped her hands together to hide the cut in the tape.

"Why do you care?"

"Aw, Beth, don't be like that. You know I actually quite like you. It's a shame you're going to die with Daniel. We could have been friends."

"In your dreams."

"No, in *your* dreams, Beth. We could have been so good together. Maybe I'll show you just how much before I deal with Daniel. He can watch. That would be amusing, don't you think?"

Bile rose to the back of her throat and she gulped. "It'll never happen. Daniel will stop you."

"Oh, I see how it is. You trust him too much. He's not the hero you think he is and very soon I'll be able to prove that to you. You'll be begging me to take you with me after you see what a loser Daniel is. But enough talk. I retrieved your mobile from the car after I escorted you to the van. I presume his number is the only one in the memory. I'm calling him now. He'll be with you soon, sweetie."

* * * *

Daniel pulled his phone out of his pocket and flipped it open. "Wyatt."

"Danny boy...how are ya?"

"What the fuck have you done with Beth?"

"Ah...so you worked it out, then. How'd you know it was me?"

"Cut the crap, Kevin. I was the one who dubbed you *The Irishman*. Now where is she?"

"Not in the mood for a friendly chat, I see. Oh well, I can understand that. She *is* a beautiful woman. Very beautiful."

"If you've touched her, I swear I'll kill you with my bare hands."

"So dramatic, Danny. Don't worry. She's safe and untouched — for now."

Daniel took a deep breath. He had to keep it together until he had a location. "Where are you? I presume you want me to come to you?"

"You're so perceptive, Daniel. I've always admired that about you, but I'm getting tired of this conversation. If you want to see her again, come alone. If you contact anyone, I'll know, and you can count on that."

"Okay, you got it. I'll come alone. Where?"

"Remember Will's cabin?"

"Where you murdered Will?"

"Danny, I'm shocked! You know I was with Beth when that happened. I can't take credit for that one, but I confess it was convenient. It managed to divert suspicion from me."

"What does this all have to do with you anyway, Kevin?"

"Ah, but that would be telling. I'll save that long story for when you get here. You have thirty minutes or I may have to start the party without you."

"What party?" Daniel's heart slammed in his chest when heard laughter over the line.

"You'll find out."

The phone line cut out.

Fuck! He checked his watch. It was only eight o'clock in the morning. Another sleepless night had him swaying on his feet, but the adrenaline rush after that conversation with Kevin had certainly woken him up. That and the fact that he was angrier than he'd ever been. He'd better get moving. He didn't have much time. He slammed the car door shut then slipped the car into reverse before flooring the accelerator, speeding backward down the lane and onto the main street. He had twenty-eight minutes to get somewhere that would normally take forty or fifty. With any luck, the traffic cops would be on their morning tea break.

* * * *

Kevin drove the van along a dirt road before finally jerking to a stop. He wrenched the door open before reaching in and grabbing Beth around the waist. She struggled to keep her hands together while he dragged her out of the van and stood her up next to him before kicking the door closed. He spun her around and pushed her toward a cabin about twenty feet away.

"Where are we?" asked Beth as she scanned her surroundings for a potential escape route.

Kevin shoved her harder, hurrying her on. "This matters because…?"

"I was just curious. Ouch!"

"Sorry, but I've decided I don't feel like talking to you right now, so shut up and you'll stay in one piece until Daniel gets here."

Fine with me. That would make it easier to hide the fact that her hands were free.

She stared at the cabin. A remnant of some previous hippie owner, it had once been multicolored. Now the many colors had faded and what were left were peeling off the weathered boards. She slowed down when she neared the door and Kevin moved in front, kicking it open with one hand anchored to her shoulder, digging in his fingers until it hurt. He pushed her in front of him again and into the corridor. "Get into that bedroom and I'll deal with you later."

She saw an open door and took a chance that it was the room he was talking about. It was. She moved in toward the old cast-iron bed and the door shut behind her. The lock turned and she was alone. She unclasped her hands and shook them, stretching out the stiffness. She focused on the old window and made a beeline for it. The wood was rotten and there were no locks that she could see. She undid the latch and tried to open it. Nothing. Applying a bit more pressure, she tried again. Still nothing. *Shit.* There was something poking out near the top of the sash. What was it? Damn, it was nailed shut. The nail protruded about an inch, and judging by the softness of the wood, she might be able to work it out of its hole. Her hand was poised over it when she heard the lock in the door turn.

She made it to the bed and sat down just in time.

The door opened and Kevin walked in with a steaming cup of coffee. "I thought you'd like some coffee since you missed breakfast."

"You're so generous. Just put it down on the dressing table over there and I'll drink it later."

"Tsk, tsk, always suspicious. You think I'd bother trying to poison you? What would be the point? I want Daniel to see what I have planned for you, so I need you alive for that."

"Alive maybe, but not necessarily conscious. Thanks, but I'll pass for now."

"Suit yourself. Your loss." He turned to leave then turned back. "Oh, and you won't have to wait long. Daniel will be here very soon. Aren't you pleased? I can hear your heart pounding from here." He laughed as he shut the door and locked her in.

She went straight for the window again and started working on the nail. She couldn't allow his words to rattle her. She was stressed enough as it was. She had to get away from there before Daniel arrived with help. It sounded simple, but whether or not she could pull it off was still to be seen.

* * * *

Daniel left his car on a neighboring property and advanced toward the cabin. The thick bushland was a useful cover as he spied the rundown buildings a short way ahead. He stopped behind the wide trunk of an old gum and crouched, opening his backpack and withdrawing his gun and a knife in a holster. He slipped a magazine into the pistol and checked the safety. He placed the gun in the back of his jeans, then lifted the cuff of his pant leg and strapped the knife to his ankle. He wished it was dark, but he had to work with what he had. He stood, then moved forward from tree to tree to stay out of sight.

When he reached the cabin, he ducked and headed to the side wall to check out the windows. He remembered from his time here two days ago that there was a bedroom on this side. Crouching, he crawled along the uneven ground, watching for obstacles and, at the same time, listening for evidence of Beth's presence. As he approached the bedroom, he heard a rattling sound coming from the window. Was Beth trying to escape? *God that woman has courage.* It was one of the reasons he'd fallen in love with her. He couldn't deny it any longer, and rather than distract him, it gave him more focus. He would get her and they would be together — if she'd have him. But that would have to wait. The rattling had stopped and he now heard voices. Kevin had come into the room and he was laughing. He took a chance and peered through the bottom corner of the window.

Kevin had grabbed Beth's hands and held them behind her back. She struggled against him as he pulled out his belt from his jeans and tied her up. She flinched as he tightened the belt. He threw her on to the bed before his hand went to her shirt and ripped it apart, exposing her bra.

Son of a bitch!

He didn't dare break the glass as it would take too long to get through the window, and it would also give Kevin a chance to draw his weapon. Instead he bolted around to the open back door and up the hallway to the room, kicking the door in. Beth screamed as Kevin placed one hand over her mouth and lowered his face to her breast. Daniel grabbed Kevin by the scruff of the neck and hauled him off her, throwing him across the floor.

He stood over him, placing a foot on Kevin's windpipe. Over his shoulder he spoke to Beth. "Did he hurt you?" He heard her short, swift breaths as she tried to calm herself. "Beth? You okay?"

Her croaky voice answered him in between intakes of breath. "He didn't hurt me. I'm fine."

"Hang on a sec while I tie this bastard up, then I'll free your hands."

Kevin gasped as the pressure on his neck increased.

"I told you I'd kill you if you touched her, but lucky for you, I find I don't have the stomach for it. I'll let the cops deal with you." He released his foot, rolled him over and straddled him while he cuffed his hands and feet with the plastic tape he pulled from his pocket.

Kevin groaned. "You've cut off the circulation! Get it off, you prick!"

"No way, you bastard. Your hands can fall off for all I care."

He went to Beth, who was still sitting on the bed. He made fast work of the belt that held her hands and he pulled her shirt together. She threw herself at him, wrapping her arms around his neck and holding on for dear life. He pulled her close with his free arm, while he kept his gun trained on Kevin and watched his every move.

"Just tell me this, Kevin. Why did you betray me?"

"Why? Because I hate you, that's why! You always were the perfect one, the one who always came first. You even beat me in rugby. Then when we finished Uni, you were still the one who won everything. You got the first job. You got promoted first. You were on the fast track to the top. I couldn't stand it any longer, so I set myself up with a little business on the side and became 'The Irishman'. You won't believe the money I have stashed away."

"I never made the connection, never suspected it was you. Even if I did give you the nickname, who thinks their best friend is a hitman? Jesus, Kevin. What happened to you?"

"Nothing happened, Daniel. I just grew smarter."

"Smart? Fuck, you were going to kill us!"

"Shame I didn't finish the job!"

Daniel pushed Beth from his arms and headed toward Kevin. "You fucking bastard!" He raised his fist to strike him but Beth grabbed his arm, preventing the blow.

"Daniel, don't bring yourself down to his level. He wants to rile you."

Daniel stared at him for about a minute, thinking about the pleasure it would give him to beat the crap out of Kevin, but she was right. It wouldn't achieve anything. He dropped his hand then held it out to Beth. "Come on, sweetheart. Let's get the hell out of here."

"You can't just leave me here!"

Daniel laughed as he and Beth walked hand in hand out of the door. "Of course I can, but don't worry, I'll send someone along to get you real soon."

"I don't think so, Daniel."

Daniel turned toward the front door and the silver-haired figure standing there. He must have walked quietly into the cabin while they were distracted with Kevin. He strode quickly toward them and grabbed Beth by the arm. He pulled her close and wrapped his arm around her neck, pressing a gun at her temple.

"Addison."

"Uncle Jack?"

"*He's* your Uncle Jack?" Daniel started to move toward them.

"Move back and drop the gun, Daniel, or I'll shoot her right here."

"Why do you want to hurt me, Uncle Jack?"

"I don't want to, Beth, but I have to. What you saw on that train could ruin me. I can't let that happen. Not after all this time. I'm sorry, Beth."

"But I can't remember anything!" She twisted in his grip but he only tightened his hold, making her cry out. Daniel inched forward.

"I can't take that chance, Beth. Get back, Daniel!"

"You saw his henchman kill Peter Wilson. He must've been worried that you recognized him somehow."

"Brilliant deduction, my dear Daniel. But you still have no idea how far this goes."

Beth closed her eyes. Was Daniel right? Had she seen someone she recognized? One of her nightmares flashed into her mind. The one where the masked man takes off his mask and shoots at her. *Oh my God! I remember!*

"What does her father have to do with this, Addison? At least let her know why this all happened."

"Her father got too nosy. He figured out I was selling information on government contracts. I had to stop him before he reported me."

"You killed my parents? You were so nice to me at the funeral, and you had that horrible man with you who followed you around. The one who reminded me of a gangster from a Mafia movie. I remember now — it was him I saw on the train!"

"Give the girl a prize! I knew you'd figure it out eventually. Lucky for me you don't get a chance to tell anyone."

"Let her go, Addison. You're just making things worse, adding her death to all the other charges that will be made against you."

Addison laughed. "Charges? What charges? I have the upper hand here. Now move back into the bedroom and let me finish what Kevin started."

"To quote your words back to you, Addison, I don't think so."

What the hell is Daniel up to? His eyes met hers for just a second and she knew. He had a plan. *Thank God.* Addison pulled her body closer to his as he cocked the trigger of the gun.

"I'll shoot her now if you don't move. Now get in there!"

"No, I think I'll just watch."

"Watch? What the fuck are you talking about?"

Beth found herself thrust toward the floor as two policemen disarmed Addison from behind and threw him face-first against the wall, pulling his arms behind him before cuffing him.

"I'm talking about you being arrested, Addison. That's what the fuck I'm talking about. Did you think I was stupid enough to come here without backup? I called the local police before I got here. I can trust *them*."

Beth stood and held out her arm to Daniel. He pulled her close and wrapped his arm around her shoulders. They walked outside toward the sunlight together. It was finally over.

Chapter Twelve

It had been two weeks since she'd returned home and Beth had spent a lot of that time re-evaluating her life. She loved Daniel. She knew that for sure now. But she also knew that more than anything she wanted to trust him to be there for the long haul. After he'd driven her home from the cabin, he'd told her she needed time to think. He kissed her goodbye and that was the last time she'd seen him.

She missed him more than she'd ever thought possible.

She walked through her front gate and checked her mailbox. Only junk mail, but she didn't really expect to get a letter from Daniel. Not unless he decided to send her a 'Dear Jane' letter. Of course, that would require a defined relationship. She had no idea what their relationship was or would be in the future. If they had a future, and she wouldn't know until Daniel made contact with her. When that was going to happen was anyone's guess. Until then, she had her memories of their time together. Every night in her lonely bed her body ached for him and every morning when she woke, her heart missed his smile and the feeling of completeness she'd felt lying in his arms.

She sauntered up the pathway to her front door and searched her bag for her key. She slid it in the lock to open the door but it opened on its own. *Shit! Someone's broken in.* She was sure she'd set the lock that morning before she'd left for work. She shuffled around in her bag and pulled out her mobile phone to call the police, but before she had a chance to dial, it rang.

"Hello?"

"Beth."

Her heart leaped. "Daniel! Thank God. I think someone has broken into my house."

"It's okay, sweetheart, it's me. I thought I'd surprise you. Come on in."

"You broke into my house?"

"Hey, I'm a spy. Force of habit. Are you coming in or do I have to come and get you?"

She didn't need another invitation. She dropped her bag and phone where she stood and ran down the hall to the living room. It was empty. "Daniel?" She tried the kitchen next. Still no Daniel. "Stop playing games, Daniel. Where are you?"

The sound of music caught her by surprise. She cocked her head to listen while she slowly made her way down the hallway, checking each room. At the end of her hall, the bedroom door was closed, but this was where the music emanated from. Smiling, she placed her eager hand on the doorknob and turned. The door opened and the delicious scent of strawberries wafted toward her. Taking a step inside, she was surprised to see the curtains drawn and the room alight with dozens of lit candles. Her antique brass bed was draped with gauze from the overhead tester and the quilt was covered in hundreds of rose petals. *Holy...wow!*

When she couldn't see Daniel, she took another step inside the room. She gasped as a blindfold covered her eyes from behind. "Daniel. You scared the living daylights out of me! What are you doing?"

She felt his warm breath in her ear as he whispered, "Relax. You're going to enjoy this."

She turned toward his face, trying to catch his mouth, but he eluded her.

"All in good time, my love."

She reached for him, but he wrapped his arms around her waist and legs and carried her to the bed, gently placing her down onto the fragrant petals.

"Daniel, I need to talk to you," she began, deliriously happy he was back and here with her now, but anxious to talk to him about their relationship.

Daniel picked up one of her hands and kissed it gently, sending shivers all over her body. He moved it over her head and before she realized what he was about, she felt soft material enclosing her wrist and something clicked. She tried to move her hand, but it was caught fast. "What are you doing, Daniel? This isn't funny!"

Before she had a chance to struggle, he'd grabbed her other hand and restrained it as well. She felt a featherlight kiss on her mouth, then the weight on the bed beside her lifted as she heard him stand.

"I'm making sure you can't get away from me while I talk to you."

She laughed at the absurdity of the notion that she would want to get away. She'd been longing for him to return ever since he'd left. "You could just ask me. I'm not going anywhere. At least take off the blindfold so I can see your face."

"Shh! You'll spoil the fun."

"What fun? Dan—" She shivered as he cupped her cheeks with warm hands and covered her mouth with his. This was no tame, gentle kiss like the first. He was devouring her as his tongue probed her lips, forcing them open then plundering her mouth as if he was starving. She moaned and burned to touch him but discovered when she pulled against the restraints that she could release herself easily. The thought that she still had control made her hotter so she chose to keep her hands where they were. She felt the buttons on her shirt being undone one by one and when Daniel was finished he spread her shirt open, baring her to the cool air. Her nipples stood to attention and she gasped.

His mouth left hers as his tongue and lips scorched a wet trail along her jaw to her ear, where he blew softly, making her whole body tingle.

"Do you like that, Beth?"

"Oh yeah…"

"That's good…but do you also like this?"

He unzipped her, pulling both her jeans and panties down her legs and off in one swift movement. The blast of cold air across her skin and the accompanying rush of sensation to her exposed body sent another burst of moisture between her legs.

"Oh God!"

"I didn't catch that, Beth. Did you like that?" he asked, as he trailed his fingers lightly over her breasts.

"Ahh…"

He grasped her nipples and rolled them back and forth. She writhed on the bed, arching her back to get even closer to him.

"Oh…" she moaned.

"What was that?" He caressed the length of her body, using one of his fingers to part her folds before he slid it inside.

She climaxed instantly. "Yes. Yes…I like it!"

His quick intake of breath told her he was getting off on this little game as much as she was. Feeling more confident in her power to arouse him, she parted her legs, exposing herself to his eyes. Though her own were covered, she nevertheless felt his gaze burning onto her entrance as she lifted her hips and invited him to sample her. She was hot, and her body begged him to taste and join her.

But instead of the expected heat, something cold, hard and wet touched her. Smooth facets slid along the line of her labia, teasing her.

"What is that?" she rasped, her voice breaking.

"It's an ice cube. I don't want you too hot just yet. We have plenty of time and I want it to last." He placed the cube inside the entrance to her vagina and held it in place. With his other hand he circled one of her nipples with another piece of ice, making it tighten almost painfully. He repeated the process with her other breast then withdrew both cubes. She waited for his next move, hearing rustling sounds of him removing his clothing, but was unable to discern what was in store for her next.

"You know, I've been thinking about doing bad things to your beautiful body ever since I saw you last, sweetheart."

"Me too…"

"Just thinking about the way you clench your body around me had me hard as a rock all day long."

"Oh yes."

He laid his firm muscular body over hers, rubbing back and forth, leaving no doubt that what he'd said was the truth.

"I thought you were going to wait?"

He thrust inside her in one swift movement, filling her to the hilt, and she gasped at the overwhelming pleasure.

"I'm sorry, love, but I can't wait. We'll do slow later." He pulled back and rammed into her again and again. The sensation of heat over cold was so erotic her body exploded, leaving her quivering and sensitized through every pore of her skin, inside and out.

"Fine by me..."

"Oh baby."

To have him take complete control of her was like nothing she'd ever experienced in her life. Despite the lack of control, she felt worshiped and adored, and oh so sexy. It was liberating to feel him taking his fill of her and she tried to let her feelings flow through her body, giving herself to him. She loved him and she was his.

Their bodies spent, they lay in each other's arms. She kissed his neck and snuggled into his shoulder. "I missed you, Daniel."

"You have no idea. Leaving you alone these past two weeks has been hell, but I wanted us to have the best chance to have a relationship. You weren't ready for it back then. Hell, I wasn't ready for it. I was still screwed up by what happened to Lisa. I just wanted to give us both time to work out what we wanted."

She released herself from the restraints and moved her hand down to his penis and stroked along its length. He groaned and grabbed her hand. "Hey...we're talking here!"

"Mmm, yes, we are, but I've got some catching up to do."

"Beth, please..." he pleaded. "I'm trying to tell you how I feel here."

"Oh, honey, you feel pretty good to me."

"Beth, be serious for a minute."

She stopped stroking and clasped him in her hand, squeezing gently. "Okay, I'm sorry. I'll be serious now."

He ran a knuckle over her cheek and tipped her chin. He smiled so tenderly it made her heart swell. "You know I love you, Beth."

She stilled her hand, and her heart started pounding a drum solo in her chest.

"You do?"

"You doubt that?"

She smiled back at him. "I love you, too, Daniel. I've known it these past few weeks, but it's only lately that I believed we could make something together. I just wasn't sure how you felt when two weeks went by and you hadn't contacted me."

He brushed a curl off her forehead and tucked it behind her ear. "You trust me to stay? I will, you know."

She gasped. He knew her fears and her joys, and gave her the best sex she'd ever dreamed of. *What's not to love?*

"Yes, Daniel, I trust you to stay."

She covered his mouth with hers for another scorching kiss and it was some time before they came up for air. She smiled wickedly to herself as their lips broke contact.

"Now, where are those handcuffs?"

About the Author

Living in a fantasy world as a child, Maggie was fascinated with telling stories. Whenever she shared her adventures of imaginary friends and saving the world from the bad guys, her mother called it 'Romancing'.

Actually it was more likely a really good ploy to get out of doing chores! Little wonder that after a life spent in many different occupations, Maggie has settled in to writing romance fiction. Her stories range from dark erotic thrillers, to fantasy tales of bondage and submission, to romantic suspense and paranormal.

Maggie Nash loves to hear from readers. You can find her contact information, website and author biography at http://www.totallybound.com.

Home of Erotic Romance

www.ingramcontent.com/pod-product-compliance
Lightning Source LLC
Chambersburg PA
CBHW020420180626
46812CB00003B/1069